War Strategy

Melissa Finger

Contents

Dedication

This book is dedicated to each person who is fighting to break unhealthy generational patterns in their family line. God has a strategy for your healing and freedom. Seek his heart, trust his plan, and connect with him through prayer, worship, and gratitude every chance you can.

Chapter 1

The room was empty except for a green chair and light coming from an unknown source. Cindy looked around unsure of what to do. As her eyes scanned the area for the source of the light, she dropped into the plush chair. It was cozy, but she didn't notice. She also didn't notice the smoke that was rolling low into the room. At first, it was white and wispy, but after a few moments the smoke turned gray, then darker, then black.

Cindy caught a glimpse of the smoke and turned toward it. The billows were rolling faster now, and it had Cindy's full attention. She tried to continue to search for the source of the dimming light as her feet instinctively pulled up into the chair to avoid the rolling smoke. The smoke must be blocking the light. In an instant, it began to feel as if Cindy was being consumed by the chair. What once was cozy began to feel like a suffocating trap. One last billow of black smoke rolled into the room, and she jumped up with a start.

Cindy blinked and looked around. She was sitting up in her bed. Sweat was beading on her skin, and she could feel her heart beating through her pajamas. She clutched the blanket and glanced at the clock on the nightstand. 3:20 a.m.

Her back gave way, and she slumped back down into the bed.

Another dream. When will they stop?

She rolled over onto her side. Her heart was still beating faster than normal.

Gabe, an angelic warrior who occasionally served with the angels assigned by the Most High God to watch over Cindy, was observing nearby. "She is still having nightmares," he commented.

"Yes," Michael, the lead angel assigned to Cindy, replied, "the Lord is revealing something to her."

"What?" Gabe inquired.

"We don't know," Rabok replied without taking his eyes off Cindy, "She hasn't shared the dreams with anyone, so we don't know the content."

"We only know they are being used by the Lord somehow because we can sense His presence while she is sleeping," Salih explained.

"She is getting what she needs, and the Lord will give us what we need as we need it," Michael interrupted, "Stay on alert! We don't want any unwelcome visitors trying to hijack her sleep."

The others nodded and followed their leader's instructions.

Rabok and Salih stayed close to Cindy as she drifted back off to sleep. As her Ministering Angels, they could aid her in rest and help her process her intense emotions. Her dreams had been more and more frequent, and she had been avoiding sleep as much as possible. Much to her despair, her sleep deprivation was making it impossible to stay awake - even after one of the dreams.

As the sun rose above Cindy's home, Rabok aided her continued rest.

Around 10:00 a.m., Cindy began to stir. As she opened her eyes, an image of the dreams flashed through her mind, and then it was gone. She sat up in bed and looked around the room. She was awake, but she wanted to be sure.

"I can't keep having nights like this," she muttered to herself.

She checked the clock, groaned, and threw her feet on the floor.

Her body felt numb, as did her mind. Her head dropped into her hands. Her eyes burned and a steady beat was pounding in the back of her head.

Why is this still happening? A voice in her head

asked, *I thought we would be better by now.*

It had been six months since Cindy had received the most powerful vision ever while sitting in her therapist's office. She knew it was God's way of giving her purpose. She just didn't know what to do with it. As she climbed out of bed and wobbled into the kitchen for coffee, she replayed parts of the vision she had seen in Mary's office.

The pictures of the strands of colorful DNA covered with grime and darkness kept cycling through her mind. She watched as the Holy Spirit cleaned each one causing them to appear stronger and brighter than ever before. There was a peacefulness about the pictures, and a curiosity as to what the vision really meant.

Cindy gave her head a shake and prepared her breakfast.

The coffee wasn't hot enough or strong enough.

She glanced out the back window as she crossed the kitchen. It was spring, and the birds were chirping outside. The blooms on her apple tree in the back were starting to appear, and she could see some of the trees in the neighbor's yard starting to produce leaves.

It's going to be a pretty spring, she thought.

Sitting at her favorite table in the kitchen, her mind drifted from this thought to that. The small wood table felt different than any of her other furniture. Somehow it represented a part of her story. It was the first piece of furniture she owned when she moved out of her parents' house. Fifty-Five Treasures was the name of the antique store where she found it, and for some reason it was a great comfort to her. She ran her fingers along the edge. It was smooth with the exception of a few divots where time had had its way with the piece. For years she had wanted to paint it a fun color, maybe a teal or a bold yellow, but she couldn't bring herself to do it. Something about the old wood, the scratches, the worn appearance, made it seem reliable. Like it had survived a lot, and if it had survived, maybe she would survive too.

As she took another sip of her coffee her eyes settled on the birdhouse just outside the kitchen window. She installed it two days ago hoping to see the bluebirds that visited her so often last year. The Lord had used bluebirds to bring her so much encouragement over the years. She didn't know when that started, really, but she liked how they made her feel close to God. Seen by God.

Her eyes squinted a bit trying to see inside the little home. No residents yet. More than anything she just wanted to know the Lord was still around. She knew He was, but she just needed it confirmed somehow.

We are still here.

I know, Cindy responded to the voice in her head, *I'm glad for that.*

No, you're not.

Well, it does remind me I'm not healed yet, but I know you are part of me, so I accept you.

It was quiet. It had been quiet a lot more than usual lately. She knew the voices in her head were simply splits of her own self, splits that were necessary to survive trauma, but she just wanted to be whole. She wanted them to all integrate into her heart so she could move forward with what God wanted her to do. Maybe that's what He was waiting for.

Maybe once I am whole God will show me what the vision means, and I can serve Him fully, she thought. *Then I can really become someone or do something big for God.*

She made her way into her bedroom and thumbed through the clothes in her closet, taking her time as she decided what to wear for the day. A light-weight blue sweater seemed like a good choice. As she pulled her sweater over her head she thought about work. It would be a long day. The first day of their big annual clearance in all departments. She only started working at the retail store about 7 months ago, so this was her first annual sale day, but she had heard stories from the other employees. She expected it to be stressful. Most of the stories were complaints of this or that bad customer, but what Cindy took away was that it would be busy, messy, and go by really fast, and she wasn't sure she could handle it on such little sleep.

I can't handle fast.

I am too tired for messy.

Can we please just stay home?

Cindy sighed, *work is necessary,* she said to herself as she slipped her feet into her shoes, *I know we can do it.*

It was quiet inside now, a different kind of quiet than earlier. Cindy felt the restlessness starting to stir deep inside. She was all too familiar with it. It would start as restlessness – which she would ignore – then it would grow to agitation mixed with deep sadness, then she would either have a meltdown or panic attack, she never knew which it would be.

Oh well, she thought as she pushed the restless feeling away and headed out the front door.

Sliding into her little Toyota felt good. It was cool outside, but the sun had warmed up the interior to a comfortable temperature. As she drove to work Michael and Gabe were nearby keeping watch on a growing gray cloud forming at Cindy's feet.

"What is it?" Gabe asked.

"Despair fueled by denial," Michael answered.

"A very harmful combination," Salih piped in, "she was eagerly waiting for the Lord to give her direction after her vision last fall, but He hasn't responded in the way she wanted. Each day now gives way to more and more despair."

"As she feels the despair, she becomes restless wanting to do something about it, but she is unsure what to do," Rabok continued, "so she just pushes the feelings down, deep down inside. The denial mechanism she developed as a child makes it easy to do."

"Can we do anything about it?" Gabe wondered.

"No, it is partially created by her own choice to deny her feelings. We have to wait on the Lord to break it's power, but not until she is ready. Thankfully, her denial mechanism doesn't work as well as it used to. The Lord has already done a great deal of healing," Hezek commented.

"Praise be to the Most High God," Michael stated.

"Praise be," the others echoed.

After a moment of reflection on the greatness of God, Gabe returned to his questions. "Then why is she still using the denial? What is she denying?"

"Her own feelings. She still struggles to feel her own heart, so despair can easily overtake her," Salih answered. It was his job to help her connect with the Holy Spirit in these emotions. "I have seen her denial mechanism shrink significantly over the years, but there is still enough denial working to block out the really sad feelings like despair, hopelessness, and a few others."

Gabe nodded as he tried to understand the complexity of the coping mechanism.

As Cindy pulled into the parking lot at work, she ignored the knot forming in her stomach and forced herself out of the car and into the building.

"Good morning, Cindy!" Brianna, a short, red-haired girl just out of high school greeted Cindy as she walked in the door. "Are you ready for today?"

"As ready as I'll ever be," Cindy replied with a smile that felt as fake as the plastic tree by the front door. Brianna didn't seem to notice. She smiled back at Cindy and then continued arranging the clothes for display.

Cindy made her way to the back room to put her purse in a locker. A few more sales associates waved and greeted her as she walked through the store. She expected to find Mrs. Watson, her supervisor, in her office. Since the day Cindy had met Mrs. Watson, she had been open and inviting. The supervisor had even revealed that she too had been on a healing journey. Cindy wasn't sure what that entailed, but she was thankful for the understanding Mrs. Watson had extended to her throughout her time at the store.

As if perfectly timed, Mrs. Watson poked her head out of the office and motioned towards Cindy.

"Good morning, Cindy," Mrs. Watson smiled, "could I see you for a minute?"

"Sure," Cindy had become more comfortable with Mrs. Watson, but it still felt awkward to work with someone who knew something of Cindy's struggle.

Cindy entered Mrs. Watson's office and sat awkwardly in one of the chairs. "Are you ready for today?" she asked her boss, forcing a smile, but still feeling fake.

"I am," Mrs. Watson returned Cindy's smile, but her smile felt warm and genuine. It put Cindy at ease, slightly. "I had a long day yesterday, so I am a bit tired today."

Cindy nodded, unsure what to say.

"I wanted to talk to you about the sales floor today," Mrs. Watson switched topics, "typically on these big sale days we have a lot more customers."

That's good, Cindy thought, *I can stay busy.*

I hate busy!

I can't do today.

"Which is good, of course, but there are always a

few customers that can get a bit more intense than others," Mrs. Watson hesitated. She glanced over at her bookshelf as if searching for something. "I'm not sure how to say this, but I thought, well, let's just say, I thought it would be good to give you a heads up on that." Her voice became more confident as if she had found whatever she was looking for. Her eyes met Cindy's, and Cindy could see the kindness that she had come to know and expect from her boss. "I know this is your first big sale day, and sometimes it can catch newer employees off guard when a customer is rude or disruptive."

"I see," Cindy said, still unsure of what to say.

"Just remember your training. Be kind and helpful if you can, but don't hesitate to find me or one of the supervisors if you need help managing a situation," she said, tilting her head as if waiting for Cindy to respond. "Does that work for you?"

"Sure," Cindy nodded and tried to smile pleasantly again. She didn't know why this was so important to call her in for a private meeting.

I've dealt with plenty of difficult customers before.

Does she think I can't handle whatever happens?

She doesn't even know us!

She knows something.

Of course, she knows something, we just don't know what.

She thinks we are stupid!

I knew this job would never last!

"I understand," Cindy stated, mostly to silence the building dialogue in her mind.

They both stood and Cindy walked towards the door. With her hand on the knob, she turned back towards Mrs. Watson, "Thanks for the heads up." She smiled again and then exited.

Out on the sales floor, Cindy headed straight for her register to begin ringing up sales. The store was starting to get busy, and she didn't want the lines to get long.

People definitely get grumpy when the lines are long!

That is their own problem!

It is their own problem until they get to the front and make it my problem!

Who cares!

I care! We need this job!

At least it is just a half-shift today.

It only takes a minute for you to do something stupid!

Cindy swatted at an invisible bug, effectively silencing the voices ramping up inside. She really didn't know if they were silent or simply buried, but either way, she didn't want to listen to them all day.

As the day drew on, customers slowly flooded every department. Cindy was stationed at her primary register in the ladies clothing department the majority of the time, but occasionally she would need to assist a newer employee in another department. She enjoyed those moments. It reminded her of the corporate management job she had two years ago. Quitting that job was one of the hardest things she had ever done but keeping that job would have been even harder.

Her entire life, Cindy had been running from her past. There is nothing she wanted more than to leave the pain and trauma of her childhood exactly there: in her childhood. But she just couldn't shake it.

That's because your trauma made you.

That can't be true! Can it?

It's not true because there was no trauma! It's all imagined and blown out of proportion.

Everyone has a hard life, what makes you so special?

Cindy heard little whimpers and soft cries in her head. She pushed it aside.

"Is this all for you today?" she asked the next lady in line. The woman was in her mid-50s and dressed a little too well for just shopping, at least in Cindy's mind.

"I guess it will have to be," the customer responded with a humph.

"Was there something else we can help you find?" Cindy felt a knot in her stomach as soon as the words left her mouth.

You're in trouble now!

We're in trouble now.

She looks scary, a little voice from deep inside whined.

"As a matter of fact, you seem to be out of the red, cashmere scarves that were in your ad," in the blink of an eye, she had pulled an ad from somewhere and was waving it in Cindy's face.

"I'm so sorry, ma'am. That was a very popular item," Cindy said, trying to sound empathetic. She reached for the lady's items to begin scanning them.

"Popular or not, you would think if you are going to advertise an item like this, you would have enough in your inventory to meet the demand!"

Cindy kept scanning her items while nodding and trying to look genuinely concerned about this woman's tragedy of not finding a scarf.

She doesn't seem to be hurting for anything.

I bet she has 20 other scarves at home!

Stupid!

"Are you even listening to me?" The woman's voice sliced through Cindy's thoughts.

The well-dressed woman was staring at her with disgust, clearly waiting for an answer to an unknown question.

"I'm so sorry we couldn't meet your expectations

today," Cindy fumbled with a pair of shoes she was ringing up, trying desperately to remember what to do in this situation.

Call a manager! Someone inside shouted.

You're such a loser. You need a manager to handle this? Just tell her to get lost!

The crying from deep inside was coming through again.

"Would you like to speak to a manager?"

Behind the woman, the line was getting long, and Cindy could tell other customers were getting agitated.

This woman is going to ruin the rest of the day for us!

Every other customer is going to be so angry!

I can't do this; I can't do this.

Cindy's knees started to buckle. She could hear the jingle of her necklace even though she wasn't moving and realized her breathing was getting heavy. Her vision was blacking out. She could no longer see the woman or the line, but she could feel their stares. Their angry, unsafe stares were penetrating her defenses. The tears were building behind that huge ball forming in her throat.

Salih moved in close to Cindy. Michael noticed the dark cloud growing at Cindy's feet and motioned two warriors to Cindy's side. Before the warriors could move, a flaming sword came out of nowhere and slashed the dark cloud which dissipated immediately. The entire angelic guard looked up and saw two towering warriors with swords move back toward a man standing in line behind the well-dressed woman.

"Excuse me."

Wait, who is that?

The voice was from a man. The voice was unfamiliar to Cindy or those inside.

Gabe raised his eyebrow as the man accompanied by the towering warriors continued to speak to the lady.

"Excuse me, ma'am?" The polite man continued as the unhappy customer turned to the side to face him. "Did I hear you say you were looking for one of the red, cashmere scarves from this morning's ad?"

Cindy forced her eyes to focus on the scene playing out in front of her.

The grumpy woman nodded an arrogant confirmation in response to his question. By now, most of the people in the line were staring at the man, the grumpy woman, and Cindy, the desperate cashier who was about to have a breakdown. To everyone's surprise, the man pulled the exact red scarf out of his cart.

"I actually have one here," the woman's eyes

flashed with a hint of anger, but before she could spew out her next statement, he continued. "I was going to buy it for my wife, but I'm starting to second guess it. Would you like to have this one?"

The woman pulled back slightly. "I'm not sure," she said, scanning him as if looking for an evil agenda of some kind.

The kind man glanced toward Cindy and gave her a subtle nod as he pushed the scarf in her direction.

Cindy's legs were barely holding her up, but this man seemed to be rescuing her. The big ball was still in her throat, but she felt her strength returning slowly, as well as her vision. At his nod, she carefully took the scarf from him and held the scanner over the tag.

"Would you like me to add this to your order?" Cindy didn't dare ring it up without the woman's approval, but she was ready the instant the woman agreed.

"I suppose," the angry customer said with another humph, "but don't think this gets the store out of trouble! I will be sending an email to your manager as soon as I get home!"

Before the woman had completed her threat, Cindy had the red scarf and the rest of the order complete. She couldn't bring herself to look at the kind stranger, but she wasn't sure why.

The woman gave Cindy her credit card and within a few minutes, the purchase was complete, and the woman was leaving the building. Cindy let out a deep breath of relief. Her knees were still wobbly, but her shift was over in fifteen minutes.

We can't do this!

What were we thinking? We can't work!

I will never be able to do anything right.

The little one inside was still crying.

Cindy forced her lungs to take a deep slow breath, and then let it out. Her eyes were closed.

Slowly a voice began to come into awareness. It was male. It was outside of her head. Her eyes began to open more out of curiosity than choice. The kind man who had given the woman the red scarf was the next customer in line and was speaking to her.

"Are you ok?" he said again.

His voice was kind and gentle. Cindy had never known a man to be kind or gentle. It felt very unsafe.

"Yes," she drew another short breath and blinked a few tears back as she picked up his items to scan them. "That was very kind. What you did for her, that was very kind." She couldn't look up. She was afraid of what she might see in his eyes. She had only ever seen evil in the eyes of men. This man felt different though. She felt peace in a way she had never felt before.

Salih stayed close to Cindy just in case her anxiety began to rise again, while the rest of the guard took note of the power of the Lord that rested with the stranger.

Something about how he had stepped in like that made her feel safe in a strange and unfamiliar way.

This is not safe!

Run! Run!

Cindy pushed the voices away with all her might.

"Would you like me to see if we have another scarf in the back?" she said without looking up from the register.

"No, no," the man said. Cindy noticed he had a slight accent, maybe he was Hispanic. "I think she needed that scarf more than my wife did." Cindy could feel his smile. He seemed pleasant and relaxed. "I will find her a different birthday gift."

Cindy gave him the total and took his credit card.

"Thank you," was all she could say. She looked up briefly, and he just smiled. Not a big intrusive smile. A knowing smile. He gave a gentle nod in return.

As she handed the card back to him, she glanced at the name on the card: Daniel Rodriguez.

Daniel, the only kind man we ever met.

There is no such thing.

Maybe not, but he did stop that woman from beating us.

Cindy froze. Beating us? Where did that come from? Is that what she was afraid of?

As if on cue, her replacement tapped her on the shoulder. "Ready to go home?"

Boy, was she! In a few moments, Cindy was checked out of her register and headed back to get her purse from her locker. Thank goodness tomorrow was therapy. She needed it!

Chapter 2

"I don't really know what happened," Cindy was talking to Mary, her therapist for many years now, "I just started to shut down, I mean completely shut down." Cindy could feel the knot starting to grow in her throat again.

"Then this nice man, well, I guess I don't really know if he is nice or not, he was a man, just a man, he offered the woman the scarf she was looking for, and then she was gone, as quick as she came."

"That sounds like it was very overwhelming," Mary commented while jotting a few notes in her book. Her glasses were still propped on her head near the silver-gray bun. Her relaxed position always made Cindy feel welcome. If Mary could be comfortable, then so could Cindy. It made it easier to talk about things.

"It was very overwhelming," Cindy continued. "I

don't know if I can keep doing this. I could have been fired!"

"Why would you have been fired?"

Why would she have been fired? Are you kidding me with that question?

Isn't it obvious? Because she is so dumb! She almost blacked out over a ridiculous red scarf!

What an idiot!

"I, um, I don't know, I just felt like it was the end of everything." For a moment Cindy realized just how out of proportion that response was to the situation. "I guess I didn't do anything wrong."

Of course, you did. It is always your fault! The voice was almost hissing from anger.

"I just realized something," Cindy started, "I have a voice inside my head that sounds just like my mom."

Mary nodded. She didn't seem surprised.

As Cindy began to describe the voice and the many different statements of blame and accusation that it spoke to her, Michael and his troops began encountering an onslaught of demonic beings.

At first, one ball of black appeared in the room, then another, then another. Revealed by the Most High God, dark entities began to appear all around. They had been pestering Cindy for longer than anyone knew. As Cindy talked, dozens began to appear, and then more began to enter from outside of the office. Daggers and weapons were drawn ready for a fight. Before they knew it, Michael and his troops were in a hand-to-hand battle with darkness on every side.

Ronan, the angelic guard assigned to Mary, and his troops were thick in the battle as well. They were not over-run, the Most High God had equipped Mary's office to withstand spiritual battles like this one, but they could certainly use some support. In that instant, Mary stopped Cindy.

"Cindy, I think this voice is part of you, but I think it is also attached to much of the evil from your past. Can we stop a moment and pray before you continue?"

Cindy nodded. She knew Mary was right. She could feel it.

"Dear Lord, we give you full authority in this office." At that, the swords of the angelic guards all began to glow. "We ask that you bind and restrain all evil in this room that is connected with Cindy's mother." Now some of the larger demons shrieked as chains appeared on their arms and legs, "and please guide us through the process of freeing Cindy from this terrible evil in her past."

The angelic guards were rounding up the rest of the darkness and keeping them in check with the power of the Most High God. The demons could not move or display any of their usual aggressive behaviors while being restrained by this Power.

Trusting in the Lord's authority in the room, Mary opened her eyes and signaled Cindy to continue.

Cindy sighed, "I think I am just now realizing how much control my mother had over me."

"How so?" Mary questioned.

"Well, she required everything to be done a certain way. There were no other options. It was her way or…" her voice trailed off.

"Or what?" Mary asked gently.

Cindy looked at her lap. Her fingers were fidgeting with the hem of her t-shirt, "it was just her way, period."

A few of the demons snickered and were instantly met with a sword to the neck. The snickering stopped.

"Cindy, I'm wondering if the woman from work yesterday may have reminded you a bit of your mother."

Cindy's face shot up as her eyes got wide, "she did!" It was a revelation to her. She could hear the little one crying inside very clearly, and for a moment she saw a picture of herself as a tiny little girl. She was carrying a blanket and bottle wandering around the living room crying.

As she spoke, a rumble could be heard by the angelic guards around the office.

"I didn't even think of that, but you are right. I felt like I was a little girl again, confused and feeling lost. My mom was yelling at me because I did something wrong."

A dark portal was now completely revealed in the little country office. Of course, Mary and Cindy could not see it, but Michael, Ronan, and the others could. At the entrance of the portal stood a large, husky-looking angel. His sword was drawn prohibiting any other entities from coming through the portal to Cindy. The Most High God sent these beings on special assignment whenever He had been given permission to block the evil, but the portal had not yet been disconnected. These beings were so empowered by the Most High God, that evil didn't dare try to move past them.

"I think you are still connected to your mother and her abusive ways," Mary commented.

"Oh, she wasn't abusive," Cindy stated abruptly. The words surprised her as she heard them come out of her mouth, "she was just picky. She needed things to be just right so we could have a good and happy life."

"Do you think that's true?" Mary wondered.

"Of course, that's not true!" Cindy almost yelled.

"Of course, it is true," Cindy stated calmly. "Mother did her best, and she expected the same from us."

"I can see part of you still feels loyal to your mother," Mary commented.

A flash of lightning could be seen deep inside the dark portal, and a chain from somewhere in the darkness connecting the portal to Cindy was slowly being revealed.

Cindy slumped back onto the couch. With her head down she continued, "I suppose so. I had to stay safe from mom. As long as I followed the rules, and did my best, then everything would be okay. I would be safe." Cindy's voice sounded young, maybe a teen. Cindy had clearly spent many years trying to please her mother in order to stay out of trouble.

"That sounds like it was difficult," Mary began, "I'm so thankful Cindy had you to help her through," Mary responded to Cindy's teen part.

"It wasn't difficult. It was what it was. As long as we did our part, everything was fine."

"Did it always work out that way? Did everything always work out fine with Cindy's mom?" Mary persisted.

"Well, we couldn't do everything just right, so of

course there were times mother had to help us."

"How did she help you?" Mary's voice was gentle and kind. She waited patiently as Cindy searched for the words.

"I don't know, she just did, that's all." A tear ran down Cindy's face.

"Cindy," Mary started, "would you like to be free from the rules and expectations that your mom put on you as a child?"

"No!" Cindy was yelling again. "That is not possible! The rules keep us safe. The rules make sure we don't get hurt." Her jaw was set, and Mary could see a vein pushing through in her neck.

"It's ok, Cindy, I'm not going to ask you to do anything unsafe." Cindy's piercing eyes examined Mary's as Mary continued to speak, "can we ask the Lord about this?"

Cindy nodded without saying a word. After another moment of glaring at Mary, she closed her eyes.

The smaller demonic entities in the room were starting to shudder a bit, but one of the larger entities chuckled as he watched Cindy close her eyes to pray. Ronan took a step closer to the dark beast that had been with Cindy her entire life. They stood eye to eye. There was a stench that came with that kind of evil. One that Ronan was familiar with, and he detested it. So did the Most High God. It was arrogant and abusive towards innocence. A thief of young trust and a manipulator of the powerless. Today, his power over Cindy would end, and they both knew it.

"Father God," Mary began to pray, "thank you for allowing us into your Heavenly Courtroom where you make rulings against evil and deliver justice for those who have been betrayed."

As Mary prayed, a picture of the Heavenly Courtroom began to form in Cindy's mind. She could see it clearly, as could each of the spiritual entities in the room. The evil responsible for the dark connection between her and her mom was standing before the Judge. Cindy always liked to see the Judge in His Courtroom. She knew this was a place to find justice and healing. Today felt a little different though. This entity had terrified her for her entire life. She was only now beginning to realize how it had been present through her mother every single day of her childhood, and now it lived with her. She shuddered at the thought. Was it even possible to be rid of this terror? Mary was still praying.

"Father God, you are the Judge over all things. You have heard the claims this entity has had on Cindy's life. But you have also heard Cindy's forgiveness towards her mother. You have heard Cindy make choices today in your Courtroom for mercy and justice."

I did? Did I make those choices? Cindy felt lost. Gaps in her short-term memory were not her favorite thing.

How much of the session did I just miss?

"I ask today, Father God," Mary continued, "that you would sever this evil from Cindy and her bloodline going forward throughout all of the generations that follow Cindy."

As she prayed, the husky, angelic guard lowered the sword that was before the dark portal and the procession of defeated evil began. One by one entities of all shapes and sizes went back into the portal, sent to wherever the Lord had decided.

"Will she be free from her mom forever?" Gabe asked his mentor Ronan.

"I can't say," Ronan responded, "only God knows the future. What I can say is that, today, right now, this evil has been bound and removed from her humanity. When God makes His ruling against evil, the evil must leave. There is no choice in the matter."

The angelic guards were dropping their swords around the room. The room was still thick with darkness, but the darkness was powerless against the Light of God. His Light was forcing every evil entity back into the portal, and there was nothing left to do but watch.

"Will my mother's voice be gone now?" Cindy asked Mary when the prayer was complete.

"I'm not sure, Cindy, let's check and see," Mary paused for a moment, "what do you hear?"

Cindy closed her eyes and listened to her own mind. "It seems quiet," she reported cautiously.

"Good," Mary jotted another note in her notebook, "I guess we will see how the week goes."

Cindy nodded in agreement, "one more thing," she added. "You know the man I told you about? Daniel, Daniel was his name."

"The one who gave the woman the red scarf?" Mary clarified.

"Yes, that's him. Well, I realized something about him while we were praying." Cindy paused trying to formulate her thoughts, "I realized he saved me from 'my mom' or the woman who was acting like my mom. No one ever did that for me before. No one ever stepped between me and my mom before."

"Wow, that must be a powerful realization for you."

"It was, but I didn't really understand that until just now," a tear rolled down Cindy's cheek, "do you mind if I take a minute and thank God for that man?"

"Sure," Mary responded with a smile.

"Father God, I don't know if you sent that man, or if he was just there, but either way, I am thankful for him. Thank you for showing me that you care. Thank you for letting him help me the way he did." Another tear rolled down her cheek. She quickly wiped it off with the back of her hand.

Mary took that as her cue and did a wrap-up prayer for their session.

As Cindy was leaving the room, she paused and turned to face Mary. "I had another thought when you were praying," Cindy started.

"Really?"

"Yes, I can't remember what it was, but it felt very powerful, in a good way."

Mary smiled, "God will remind you when the time is right."

"I figured you would say that," Cindy grinned, "but I wanted you to know."

"I know that happens a lot," Mary started. "Of course, you didn't really have time to write it down in session before it left your mind, but it may be helpful to keep a notepad with you - in your car or by your bed - so you can write down thoughts as they come to your mind."

Mary had suggested this before, but Cindy had never been one for writing things down.

Maybe I should try it?

With a simple nod, Cindy turned and left the room, headed to her car.

As Michael started behind her, he glanced back at where the portal was closing and disappearing out of view. He paused as he caught a glimpse of Cindy's family farmhouse inside the portal. It was surrounded by darkness, but it was undeniably the farmhouse. Then he realized the chain was still visible coming out of the portal toward Cindy. "Interesting," he mumbled, "I know you see that Lord God; I trust your timing with disconnecting it." He then caught up with Cindy and the rest of the angelic guard in the parking lot.

Fifty miles outside of town, something was shifting. A huge black portal hovering over a large farmhouse began to drip darkness over the land. Like a sewer backing up, the stench from the portal spewed over the fields. A bolt of lightning struck from the inside of the portal to a tree on the vast land surrounding the farmhouse. The tree crashed to the ground sending sticks, large branches, and leaves in all directions.

"What was that?" Darlene asked her husband with a start.

Darlene was in her 60s. Her hair and clothes were always perfect, and her makeup was done even if she wasn't leaving the house. As she sat up in her chair, she tilted her head to listen for any other sounds.

"I don't know, dear," her husband didn't look up from his phone, "I'm sure it is nothing."

"I'm sure it is something," she said with irritation. She got up and headed to the window. "I don't see anything, but I know something happened. I felt it."

Her husband didn't respond.

"Are you listening to me?" She stood by the window with one hand on her hip.

"I'm sure it is fine," he said without looking up.

She scowled at him for a moment and then turned her attention back to the window and stared out into the field of trees of grass.

Back in town, Cindy was just leaving the grocery store. At Mary's request she had purchased a notebook to keep handy along with a few groceries she was needing for home. She felt lighter. The sun even seemed a little brighter, like she had been wearing sunglasses her whole life and they were finally off. She didn't usually go anywhere but home after counseling, but today was different. She was different.

Maybe God is going to start showing me

whatever he meant by that vision he gave me months ago, she thought.

She waited a moment for the internal rebuttal.

There was none.

"Hmm," she said softly.

When she arrived home, she began preparing dinner. The day had flown by. She wasn't really sure where the time went, but that was normal for counseling days. She typically lost time, not knowing where exactly she had been or what exactly she had done. It was very unsettling at times, but she could usually brush off that feeling.

"Did you check the perimeter?" Michael was asking Hezek.

"Yes, no changes," Hezek reported. As he started back, he hesitated and turned back to Michael, "actually, there was one change," he started, "the trees outback actually seem to have bloomed since we left this morning."

"Interesting," Michael responded, "thank you, you may take your post."

Hezek paused as if he was going to ask a question, but then decided otherwise and returned to his post near the door of the kitchen where Cindy was working on dinner.

Today was interesting, Cindy thought.

There is something different tonight.

Nothing will ever be different.

Tonight there is.

Cindy was used to her thoughts going back and forth and over and over, but there was a distinct change in her thought pattern this evening. *Less internal aggression somehow,* she pondered.

She finished dinner and headed to bed. The exhaustion was taking over, and she wanted to get as much sleep as possible before her shift at work tomorrow. The weekend was coming, and she wanted to enjoy it while her internal system seemed to be a little quieter. As she settled into bed, she began to feel the tinge of fear start to grip her heart.

The dreams! I don't want the dreams!

Flashes of the nightmares Cindy experienced time and time again whipped through her mind, but just as quickly as the flashes started, another thought came out of nowhere. Cindy sat up in bed with a start.

"I remember!" she smiled.

"At the end of the session, Jesus told us he would be with us to the ends of the earth," Cindy whispered to her parts as she settled back under the blankets. "So we don't have to be afraid." She smiled as she closed her eyes.

The presence of God covered her and surrounded her home as she drifted off to sleep.

Zral and Abel, two of the worshiping angels stationed with Michael's troops, sang slow melodies to the Most High God throughout the evening. As the praise rose from Cindy's home, she slept without nightmares, without any dreams really. It was simply peaceful, and that was just what she needed.

At the edge of town, the scene was quite different though. Darlene was screaming at her husband about unpaid bills and troubles at church. Her husband was quiet, he didn't respond, and he didn't try to stop her. Outside of their farmhouse, the stench from the dripping portal was getting stronger and covering the land more and more with each passing hour.

Chapter 3

Friday morning came with a start. As Cindy's alarm blared in her room, her eyes sprung open. She could feel her heart beating, but it wasn't pounding like the dreams had returned. It was as if she felt life in her chest, in her body. It was a new sensation, and, although it was odd, Cindy liked it.

Her hand reached for her phone to dismiss the morning chimes.

Silence.

She could hear rain tapping on the roof above her. The sound of the rain typically brought mixed feelings for Cindy. She enjoyed sitting by the fireplace, drinking something hot, and listening to the gentle pitter-patter most of the time. Other times though, she would see dark, raging storm clouds in her mind, and the tapping of the raindrops would sound more like hammers to her soul. Today was somewhere in the middle.

She listened for another moment, and then decided it was time to get moving.

Michael's troops were headed back from their morning perimeter check with nothing new to report. The worshiping angels were praising God for the rain to refresh the earth and the beauty in the cycle of the seasons. Rabok and Salih were near Cindy, as usual, while enjoying the worship being lifted to the Most High God.

For Cindy, the morning moved by at a normal pace. Coffee and breakfast, shower and dress for work, then sit for a few minutes in the living room and make a plan for the day. Work would take up most of the day, of course, but the evening was the tricky part. It didn't really seem to matter what she planned for the evening, it rarely happened. In fact, she couldn't remember what she had done one single evening in a very long time.

There is a reason.

A reason for what?

A reason you don't remember the even. . .

She wouldn't let that last thought finish. She quickly got up, found her purse and keys, and headed to the door.

The rain met her at the edge of the porch. It wasn't the gentle kind today. A bit cold and harsh. She heard thunder in the distance and decided to grab an umbrella instead of running for it like usual.

Where did I leave that umbrella?

I don't know.

Why can't I just put things back in the same place?

Normally there would be a snide comment in a situation like this, but there was none.

"Am I stupid?" She decided to bait herself a little or maybe she just missed the sarcastic voice that always kept her in place.

Still nothing.

She found the umbrella in the bedroom closet of all places and headed back out to the car.

The umbrella was successful in keeping her hair dry, but her shoes and pant legs were soaked.

Good thing I work in retail, she thought, *I can get something different and change if this doesn't dry off.*

She set the heat in the car to high and started down the road. Today would be the third day of the big annual sale. It ran through the weekend, but she only had to work today and tomorrow. Scenes from the red scarf incident ran through her mind for the remainder of the drive. It didn't carry the punch with it that she thought it should. It wasn't pleasant to think about, but it didn't make her nauseous or give her a headache. Just thinking about it was interesting.

As she pulled into the parking lot, she could see

the store was already busy. She parked at the far end of the lot, as employees were supposed to do, and turned the car engine off.

Michael had already sent out the guard to do the usual checks. Worshiping angels were at a low hum singing praises of adoration to the Lord. Rabok and Salih were ready if needed, but Cindy's heart was steady, and her mind was more still than usual.

"God," Cindy started while looking out at the storm covering the small town, "I don't know what today will bring, but I believe you are with me." Thunder cracked overhead, and she jumped with a start. After a deep breath, she continued, "I know you are keeping me safe. I don't know how, and part of me feels like it is too good to be true, but I trust you." She could feel a lump swelling in her throat. She didn't know if it was grateful tears or sad tears, but she didn't want to wait to find out. She pushed the lump back down and gathered her things.

The dash across the parking lot with potholes and wind-blown rain did nothing for her outfit. She was shaking her umbrella off as she walked through the doors. Brianna was there with her customary greeting. Mrs. Watson was crossing the floor and gave a polite nod in Cindy's direction. Several customers saw her weather-worn appearance and gave knowing smiles. One even pointed to her own wet shoes and giggled.

Normally, this much attention would make Cindy squirm so badly she would feel like she was coming out of her skin. Today wasn't like that. She didn't like all the attention, but it didn't make her feel like she was going to die.

Thankfully, she had been eyeing a pair of black dress pants and a cute spring top for the last couple of weeks. So, she grabbed a few things and headed to the back. She would save the tags and ring them up later.

Within fifteen minutes she was out on the floor getting ready to ring up her first customer of the day and look who it was!

"Angela!" Cindy greeted her friend warmly. The happy tone in her own voice startled her. "What are you doing here?"

Angela piled a small collection of clothes and accessories on the counter, "I always try to stop by for this sale! I have found some great deals over the years." She was smiling big, in her usual way. "I haven't seen you at church for a while." She commented, "Is everything okay?"

Angela was Cindy's pastor's wife and had become sort of a friend over the past year. Cindy wasn't sure how it happened. She didn't really have many friends, but Angela had always been kind, and Cindy liked that. Despite Angela's kindness, Cindy was always so fearful that she would ruin things with Angela that sometimes it made it hard to connect with her.

"Yes," Cindy started searching for an adequate response for missing church while avoiding eye contact and scanning Angela's selections. "I have just been busy," was all she said.

"Well, I have missed seeing you!"

Cindy knew it was true, but she couldn't allow herself to believe it. She scanned the last item and gave Angela the total.

Angela handed Cindy her credit card, "so has the sale week been crazy?"

"Not bad," Cindy mustered a smile, but she was starting to feel a little bad. She felt guilty for not going to church, and now she felt guilty for saying she was too busy. She wasn't.

"Well, have a good rest of your day! I'll be praying for peace for you in all this sale madness!" Angela laughed her light-hearted laugh. Cindy forced a smile and a ridiculous-looking wave goodbye. If Angela noticed how awkward she was, she didn't show it.

One by one, Cindy helped customers check out. The day went relatively smoothly. Part of her was on alert for the red scarf lady, but she never saw her.

In the back of her mind, she wondered if she would see Daniel again today. She really didn't want to. She was afraid he would just turn out to be a regular man, the kind she had always known, and that the specialness of what happened on Wednesday would be ruined. But she never saw him.

As she was leaving for the day, she realized how the workday felt completely different than any other day had. She was still really concerned about doing a good job – she definitely didn't want to lose this job – but she didn't feel like she was walking in fear all day. She was just a normal lady doing a regular job. It was a strange feeling, and she wasn't sure if she liked it. On one hand, she felt more free than she had ever felt before, but on the other hand, she felt vulnerable and unsafe.

Normal? What part of you is normal?

Cindy winced.

If people only knew.

The last remark started to bring shame, but then Cindy remembered the words of the Lord from the end of her session, "I am with you to the ends of the earth." For just a moment Cindy felt the freedom this statement gave her. It was just enough for the shame to melt away.

He is with me. She smiled and walked toward the door.

She held her umbrella to her side as she headed across the parking lot. The rain had mostly stopped. The sun was setting, and the sky was darker than when she arrived in the morning. The storm clouds were persisting though. They seemed ominous and looming even closer to the ground than earlier, but very little rain was falling from them. She started the car and pulled out on the main road. On the horizon, she could see what was left of the sun breaking through the dark clouds. It looked like freedom. A tunnel of darkness leading to the light. She wanted the light, so she drove for it.

Kaleb was on patrol ahead of the car and darted back with a message for Michael. "There is something brewing ahead. I'm not sure if it is related to Cindy or not, but I thought you should know."

"Good work, Kaleb, thank you," Michael responded.

The other warriors drew their swords just in case.

As Cindy was drawing closer to the edge of the storm, her thoughts of the conflict between freedom and safety were escalating. She had carried pain with her for her entire life. The conflict between where she was and where she wanted to be seemed to be more than she could bear. The push and pull between freedom and vulnerability. On one hand, she desperately desired to be free. She wanted to be free of the pain and sorrow of her past. She didn't want her trauma; she didn't like her story or what it made her into.

We can't be free.

Our trauma will always be part of us.

Cindy felt the despair start to take over.

The conflict….to be free is all she ever wanted. She never thought it was possible until the past couple of years, but now that it seemed like it might be possible, it was actually terrifying. To be free meant to be vulnerable. It meant to not know what was safe or unsafe. How could she ever not know about the horrors possible in this world?

She reached the edge of the storm and pulled her car over to the side. The freedom that was just beyond the edge of darkness was what she had dreamed of, but was she really strong enough to cross the line? What if the light actually killed her instead of freeing her?

Cindy glanced back over her shoulder. She could see the small town she had lived in her entire adult life in the distance. Rain was starting to pour out of the clouds in some spots, but everything looked dark and gloomy. In spite of its appearance, it felt familiar and comfortable. She turned and looked ahead of the car. More clouds were clearing now, and she was practically in the sunlight. It was all so different. In the darkness, fear was her companion. In the light, who would she have?

Tears began to run down Cindy's face. There were no sounds, no heaves of emotion, just tears. She silently put the car into drive, turned around, and headed home.

"Whatever was brewing, it is nearby," Kaleb reported as they followed Cindy back to town.

Michael's only response was a nod.

Sitting on her couch in the living room, Cindy could hear what was left of the rain dripping from the gutters outside. A few birds chirped here and there presumably heading for their evening roost. Cindy sat with her knees pulled up tight to her chest and wrapped in a worn yellow blanket. She had never liked the color yellow, but somehow tonight it seemed appropriate.

A colleague had given her the fluffy, yellow blanket as part of a special going away gift when Cindy left her corporate job. It was in a nice basket with some candles and chocolates and a couple of fiction books that she had never taken the time to read. The basket looked pretty, and the gifts were thoughtful, but the gift just made her feel like a worse failure.

Now the yellow of the blanket reminded her of

the sun on the edge of the storm. It was the freedom she could never have. She was a prisoner to the storm. She knew it, and the storm knew it.

Unbeknownst to Cindy, Michael and the entire angelic guard were thick in battle all around her. What had been brewing at the edge of the storm was a claim for Cindy's soul. Her despair and denial had attracted it, and now the Lord's army was fighting for her life.

Zral and Abel sang songs of God's greatness in battle, and Rabok and Salih were close to Cindy's heart. The despair that had been taunting her was now consuming her. There wasn't much Rabok or Salih could do. All they could do was be ready. They were watching for any glimmer, any sudden shift in the despair so they could reach her heart and the Holy Spirit could do his work.

"Why is this so hard?" Gabe asked as he battled two demons at the same time.

Michael, who never missed an opportunity to educate, replied. "She is choosing this despair. She doesn't want to, but it feels like her only choice, and her choice gives it power."

"Why? After all the Lord has shown her?" He speared two demons through the side who had just entered the room without losing a step fighting the two in front of him.

Michael gouged a large entity that had been slowly moving closer to Cindy and turned to give Gabe a quick response, "she is afraid, and while freedom is always better, it is completely unknown to her, her entire life everything unknown has been bad. It can seem like there is no choice when it seems your only two choices are a known evil or an unknown."

Gabe nodded.

"The lie is that she has no choice, but she does. It is the power of her choice that will defeat the despair," Michael added.

There was no more time for talking as the battle now took the full attention of both warriors.

There is no way out.

Nothing can be better.

There is no better.

This is all there will ever be.

Darkness now gripped Cindy's heart as voices of despair whispered in her ears.

I'm scared, a little voice whimpered.

Cindy needed the predictability of the storm. She needed the pressure of the storm. How else would she know what to do? How else could she survive? As the last thoughts of despair flooded her mind, she wept. She wept like she hadn't in years. The pain and sorrow of all she had endured were too much, and now the hopelessness of her own choices keeping her trapped was overtaking her heart and her mind.

"Stand your ground," Michael commanded the troops as the pressure from despair began to increase. "The Most High God will be our strength!"

At that, the worshiping angels sang louder and stronger, and Rabok and Salih pressed in a little closer to Cindy.

As Cindy's tears began to run dry, her eyes became heavy, and sleep overcame her.

"She is asleep," Rabok stated to no one in particular.

"Stay on alert," Michael ordered him.

Rabok and Salih were still waiting for a moment, a flicker of an opening to her heart.

As the battle raged all around her, Cindy's mind drifted into a deep, deep sleep.

The green chair appeared first. Cindy felt weak throughout her entire body. It was easy to sink into the chair, and this time, she wasn't even interested in the light that was shining in the distance. She pulled her feet into the chair. Her chin was down, and her gaze drifted across the floor. She felt weightless here. Almost as if she was floating. There was nothing to fear because there was nothing to care about.

Silently, the dark smoke began to fill the room as it had in so many dreams before. Cindy just watched as it danced along the tiles and made its way up higher and higher. There was no fear because there was no pain. There was nothing here. She was nothing here, so nothing mattered.

The battle in the living room was growing stronger. A few warriors had joined the small group. Michael was unsure how they had come to fight, but he was grateful.

Each guard was standing their ground now, the enemy was not able to advance any farther, but the fight was still intense as hand-to-hand combat took place in every space around Cindy. Rabok and Salih never looked up, they kept their eyes focused on Cindy waiting for a signal from her heart that the battle was shifting.

The smoke felt warm as it reached Cindy's feet. There was a strange comfort in it. As it continued to rise, so did the heat. The comfort began to sting and then burn. The thickness of the smoke was now very heavy and the pressure on Cindy's skin was increasing. Her heart began to beat faster, and her breath became short. Panic started to overtake her.

Her body was tense as her eyes darted around the room, now desperate for help. All she could see was the smoke rising, rising, consuming nearly all that was in sight.

"Jesus," she muttered just before the smoke consumed her.

"There it is!" shouted Rabok as a flash of light shot from Cindy's heart.

Like lightning, Salih's sword connected to the light.

"Hold it!" Michael shouted from somewhere across the room. "She is choosing Jesus; she is choosing to fight!"

Cindy began to wriggle a bit in the green chair as the smoke started to pull away from her body.

The light around Salih's sword was very slowly growing.

Cindy was struggling to breathe under the cover of the dark smoke, but her feet were free now.

The darkness around Salih's sword was slowly moving away from the growing light.

Cindy pushed herself to her feet. Her face was now just above the smoke. "Jesus, help me," she said with a little more strength than before.

Rabok was trying to bring rest to her as she twitched and cringed in her sleep. The darkness in her living room shrieked and recoiled just enough that Michael and his troops were able to push a strong counterattack against them.

"Jesus," Cindy said one more time. Darkness fell. Her body flattened on the green couch in her living room. The dream had ended. The yellow blanket slid to the floor as Salih's sword completely dissolved the darkness that was surrounding her.

The power of the Holy Spirit began to fill the room. Demons began to flee, and darkness was sucked out of the home.

Michael and his troops stood with their swords pointed to the ground. Just like that the battle was over, but they were too exhausted to move. One by one, they turned their eyes towards heaven and joined Zral and Abel in songs of praise and gratitude for deliverance.

Rabok and Salih stayed close to Cindy the rest of the night while the Holy Spirit ministered to her in her sleep.

Eventually, the warriors re-sheathed their swords and took their positions around the home. The peace of God was filling the space and refreshing the strength of the angelic guard. No one spoke. The moment was both holy and full of rest.

For the rest of the night, all that could be heard was the low hum of the worshippers and the steady breathing of Cindy.

Chapter 4

The sun was bright as it lit up Cindy's bedroom. It was Sunday morning somehow. She couldn't really remember the past few days. The last thing she remembered was sitting in Mary's office on Thursday talking about work and her mom.

Mom.

Why did you have to mention her?

Cindy ignored the inner dialogue and swung her feet over the edge of the bed. For a moment a picture of a thunderstorm flashed through her mind, but she dismissed it and reached for her phone.

"Do you think she will make it to church today?" Gabe asked no one in particular.

"It is hard to say," Rabok responded, "after the battle ended Friday night, her sleep has been much better."

"I agree," affirmed Michael, "Although the battle on Friday night was decisive in her choice for the

Lord's help, she has not completely rejected despair as of yet."

"I admire her strength," Hezek said.

"She carries the strength of the Lord with her, she just isn't fully aware of it yet." Michael paused and then asked, "any indication the nightmare returned last night?"

"No," Salih replied, "I hope we have seen the last of it."

Michael agreed.

Cindy had made her way into the kitchen and was sitting at the table munching on a piece of toast while staring out the window.

Outside her window, the little tree she had planted was now bursting with leaves and seemed so alive.

When did that happen, she wondered, *last I noticed it was just empty branches. Oh well,* she shrugged.

She listened internally for a moment. There were a few voices, but none she could make out. It was an unusually quiet morning.

Maybe today will be ok after all.

Maybe.

She assumed work had gone okay yesterday since she woke up in a decent mood. In fact, since the morning had been so much better than Cindy had anticipated, she decided to go to church. The small-town church she attended had recently added a "late service" to the Sunday morning lineup. It was so strange to have more than one Sunday service to choose from. She had heard that bigger churches in big cities would sometimes have three or four weekend services. She couldn't even imagine that. Still, being able to sleep in a little and then go to church was very appealing, so she decided to try the "late service" to see what it was all about.

On the way to church, her spiritual entourage was close by. The warfare was minimal, which was unusual for a Sunday.

As Cindy pulled into the parking lot, the traffic was unusually busy. Some cars were leaving, and others were coming. It seemed a bit confusing. Her Toyota was carefully nudging into the lot as Cindy tried to navigate to her usual parking spot.

Useless.

Just go home.

No one wants to be here anyways.

I do.

The resistance made Cindy even more determined to get inside. She needed something from God today. She didn't know what, but she craved it. Today was one of the few times she had the strength to push toward a craving of any kind, so she brushed the contrary voices aside and forged ahead.

Finally, at her parking spot, she turned the car off and sighed a deep sigh of relief.

I made it! She thought as she shifted her car into park.

Angelic voices were praising God from inside the little church. Zral and Abel had already joined the melody from the car. It was clear the presence of God had been resting on the place all morning.

Cindy sat in her car watching the people enter. For her, it was quiet. She couldn't hear the angels singing. She couldn't hear the voices of the people heading into church. It was just the sound of her own breathing. It felt peaceful and good.

She was pleased to have made it to her special parking spot. It was important to her because she could easily see the entrance without easily being seen by everyone passing by. It gave her a chance to assess the safety of the day, to get a feel for whom she might see inside, and to decide if she would actually go in or not. More times than not, this view had led her to leave a few minutes after service started. It seemed there was always a reason to feel unsafe, but today, she was determined to push through all her feelings. She felt a battle and although she didn't understand it, she knew God was the only way she would find victory.

As she sat in her car, she saw many familiar faces approaching the building. Tom and Cathy, an older couple who had been attending the church since before Cindy could remember, were walking hand in hand toward the front doors. Sarah and her bunch of three young children were unloading out of a minivan. Cindy had helped Sarah find a job several years ago after her husband had died of cancer.

I wonder if she still works for the seamstress.

Of course, she does. She can probably hold a job way better than you can.

Cindy sighed again and pushed the voices away.

A couple she didn't recognize was crossing the parking lot one row in front of her. They were young, maybe mid 20's. She was wearing heels, and a skirt with a flower top, and he was wearing khakis with a button-down shirt and a tie. They seemed a little over-dressed for this country church.

Her eyes scanned the parking lot one more time before she finally decided to get out of the car.

I can't believe I am actually going to do this!

This is a BAD idea!

I'm nervous.

"I'm nervous too," Cindy responded to the last voice she heard, "but I also just have this strange feeling that God wants us here today. He has done so much for me, and I want to be able to honor him at least this one time."

She pushed herself out of the car, shut the door firmly, and headed to the building. Her right hand was clutching her keys and her other hand was wrapped tightly around her purse strap. Somehow it was comforting to have these items close.

As she approached the front door of the church, waves of different emotions tried to surface. She didn't understand what emotions they were or why they were there, so she closed her eyes and shoved them as deep down as possible. Her legs wobbled a bit, and she caught herself on the door of the church. She took a deep breath to ground herself and then opened her eyes.

The inside of the church was just as she remembered. The décor was updated almost two years ago to rescue the church from the 1980s where it had been held hostage for several decades. It took weeks to get the paint smells out of the building. This was around the time she was recovering from quitting her job. It had taken months to be able to leave her home again for more than just a quick grocery run, and then they started the church remodel. The smell and mess were too much for her, and she missed months of services. The spiral she felt over that twelve-month period was debilitating.

Angela, the pastor's wife, was the only good thing to come from that. Angela had initially visited with Cindy when she went in to tell the church the paint smell was too overwhelming for her to attend. Cindy remembered being terrified that she would be kicked out of the church for her complaint, but she wasn't. Angela took the time to listen to her concerns and talked with her for almost an hour. When Cindy left the church that day, she felt heard and seen – new feelings that were strange and unsure. Since then, Angela had taken the initiative more than once to get together with Cindy. It was nice, and terrifying, and needed, and probably many other things that Cindy didn't want to think about.

Today though, Cindy was thankful to be able to walk through the doors of the church. She made her way toward her usual seat. Easy in and easy out. That was always the plan.

Michael and the troops were greeted with nods by many of the angels in and around the building. It was refreshing and empowering to be in such a strong presence of the Lord. Safety was felt here today by all.

As the service began, Cindy noticed very few differences from the regular morning service. The clock at the back of the sanctuary was the only indicator that this was a different service. Her internal system seemed to have settled into the church routine as well. Her internal voices had been effectively silenced or were hiding or buried somewhere.

As the pastor approached the front, Cindy stiffened slightly. He was a nice man, but he was still a man. It was always hard to trust men. Today he brought his wife out on the platform with him. Cindy relaxed slightly. She liked Angela, and her presence brought some ease to Cindy's mind. Cindy had made a complete idiot of herself several times when she was with Angela, and yet, the pastor's wife didn't seem to mind or notice. She also listened well.

"Our new Connections Pastor has a special announcement for us today," the pastor was saying.

Connections Pastor? What is that?

They had never had a Connections Pastor before. But it had been a while since Cindy had attended.

A man walked up on the stage, took the microphone, and began to speak. The second Cindy heard his voice, she froze in her seat.

He is here!

How can he be here?

This does not feel safe!

Did he know I would be here?

What is happening?

As she stared at the man speaking on the stage, she didn't need to know his name. She knew it. Daniel Rodriguez.

How was the red scarf man at my church?

Internal parts began to stir a bit.

Rabok and Salih sensed her panic and worry. They were immediately joined by a few other ministering angels who began to make a way for the Holy Spirit to minister to Cindy's heart and mind.

I feel scared.

But I don't feel scared, Cindy responded to the voice in her head. *In fact, I feel kind of peaceful.* A contradiction in emotion was normal for Cindy in many ways, but fear was rarely contradicted. Feeling the sense of the Lord's presence allowed her to linger in the service.

The worshiping angels were still singing across the room. The warrior angels were at ease. There was no spiritual danger in this place.

Cindy was unsure how to respond to the sudden interjection of this man she had met at her job.

Will he recognize me?

Will I need to talk to him?

Thoughts swirled through her mind. She heard nothing else that was said by the red scarf man, but she was able to sit through the rest of the service. She didn't want to cause a scene, and it felt that if she stood, she would run and not walk out. The sensible thing would be to wait and make a quick exit at the end of the service to avoid any awkward encounters.

The sermon took too long, and Cindy felt light-headed and weak. As the pastor was saying the final prayer, she slowly rose, gathered her things, and quickly walked to the back door.

Too late! A part yelled as they approached the back door hoping to not be noticed.

Daniel was already there prepared to greet each person as they left.

That is a good idea if he is going to be a Connection's Pastor – whatever that is.

I'm scared!

Can we get by him?

Before Cindy could come up with a Plan B, she was face to face with the red scarf man.

"Good morning!" He said with that familiar smile. He reached his hand out to shake Cindy's. She hesitated for a second and then decided to be polite and shake his hand. Before she knew it, she was in a full hug.

Cindy could feel her heart beating fast.

Danger! Danger!

This isn't safe!

She could see her car in the parking lot over his

shoulder, and all she wanted to do was to escape to her car and drive and drive and drive as far away as possible. But just when she thought her brain was going to explode from fear, she felt a wave of peace come over her. It was so sudden, it was disorientating. She felt a strange warmth deep in her heart. It was completely unfamiliar to her.

Is this what safe feels like? Someone asked in a timid voice.

NO! NO! This is not safe! There is no such thing as safe!

The hug itself only lasted a second or two, but to Cindy, the world stood still. As Daniel released her from the big bear hug, she glanced into his eyes as she pulled away.

It can't be. She thought.

It was more than she could take, and she practically ran to the car. She didn't say a word to him, but she thought she heard him saying something as she fled.

In a matter of minutes, she was out of the parking lot and a mile down the road.

"Is she okay?" Gabe asked. It was unusual to see her in such turmoil with no evil present.

"She is," was all Michael said. His smile said he knew more than he was saying.

Cindy's mind raced with thoughts and feelings and images. She didn't understand what was going on; she couldn't sort out her own thoughts.

Thoughts of feeling safe collided with beliefs set against safety. She knew God wanted her to be safe, but she didn't believe it was ever possible, not really. If safety did exist, well it just couldn't!

The sound of her stomach growling interrupted her thoughts.

I'm so hungry.

Me too.

At least we can eat, she responded to herself.

She pulled into a highway gas station miles from her town. There was a restaurant attached, and it seemed as good a place as any to rest. As she sat at the table staring at the menu, her mind felt blank, numb. The waitress came and went. Cindy knew she had ordered, but she didn't know what. When the food came, she ate it without tasting a single bite. Then she made her way out to her car. She couldn't remember if she had filled the car with gas yet or not, so she started it to see.

A full tank, she said to herself.

She sat behind the wheel with the car running. The morning was such a mix.

Who is this Daniel?

Did we really see Jesus in his eyes?

How did that hug feel so safe?

Her mind was starting to fill with thoughts again,

but this time slower, steadier.

Safe isn't real! Someone insisted.

But what if it is real? What if someone could be safe?

Ridiculous!

Jesus is safe.

No one is safe. Period.

Cindy was all too familiar with this line of thinking. Rarely did it get resolved on her own. She would file this experience away and bring it up with Mary on Thursday. Before she pulled out of the gas station she put her home address in the GPS on her phone, and off she went.

* * * * * * * * * * * * * * * * * * *

At the family farmhouse, Darlene was entering the living room with a cup of coffee in one hand and a piece of mail in the other. "We really do need to talk about this," she said as she dropped the letter on the coffee table in front of her husband.

"Not now, Darlene," came the cold response.

"It's not going away you know," she waited, but he didn't even look up from his phone. "The attorney called again yesterday and said this has to be dealt with now."

Still no response.

"I don't know why I even bother with you!"

Darlene shouted as she slammed her coffee cup on the table. "We are going to lose everything! Are you going to do anything about it?" her hands were on her hips now and her face was flushed with anger.

"Are you even listening to me?" she shouted.

Her husband quietly set his phone down and looked up at her. His face was calm, almost amused. He studied her and her angry pose for a moment.

"Well?" she pushed, not bothered by his demeaning gaze.

"When I am ready to talk about it, I will talk about it," he stood and headed out of the room. Without looking back, he added, "do not bring it up again."

Darlene screamed and threw her coffee cup against the wall before she stormed back into the kitchen.

$$* *$$

The day had been long, and Cindy was glad to be back in her house. It felt like she spent her entire life in her house or in her car.

And work, we must go to work.

Yes, work too, but I don't always remember work, so that doesn't count.

The last thought made Cindy grimace a bit. She

hated not remembering days of her life. It made her feel cheated, and embarrassed, and afraid, and probably a bunch of other emotions she was unaware of.

She smiled as she realized that was something Mary would probably bring up. All the emotions she was unaware of.

She's not wrong.

I know, I know.

Cindy went through her usual evening routine. As she thought about Angela, Daniel, and Mary, she began to realize how many people God was bringing into her life. Even Mrs. Watson was someone who felt sent by God. Cindy didn't even know what it meant for someone to be "sent by God," but each of these people felt different than anyone had ever felt before.

She drank a cup of decaf coffee while heading into her bedroom.

The more she thought about each of them, the more she realized what they had in common. With each person, she felt seen. Normally, that would terrify her, but with these people it never did. It was a little scary at times how Mary always knew what was happening before Cindy did, and she still wasn't entirely comfortable with her employer knowing she was in counseling, but somehow it still felt safe.

There's that word again.

I know. I'm sorry.

God was supporting her in a way she didn't understand. It was something she had desperately needed but never dared to ask for. Today seeing Jesus in Daniel's eyes, well that was something beyond her comprehension.

Can we figure it out tomorrow? I'm tired. A young voice responded.

Cindy smiled. A request she could easily meet. She changed for bed and after one more sip, took her coffee cup back to the kitchen.

"How is the perimeter?" Michael asked Kaleb as he returned from an inspection.

"All clear," he reported. "How do you think the night will go?"

While angels did not know the future, Michael had been with Cindy for a very long time, and he usually knew what would happen and when. His guard relied on his wisdom in this regard.

"I'm not sure." Michael studied Cindy for a moment as she slid into bed and reached to turn her lamp off. Then he looked around the room taking in each item as if it was something new to inspect. After a moment he added, "much has changed over the past few days. We should stay on alert throughout the night in case the dreams return." At that, he moved into his position by the bedroom door for the night.

The rest of the guards followed suit and took their positions. The only sounds in the room were the songs of the worshiping angels and a slight pitter-patter of rain from a new storm passing through.

* *

As Monday morning came, the storm had fully moved out of the area. The sun was starting to spread across the ground, waking up the birds and bugs, who were coming alive more and more each day. Spring had always been a mild season in her small town, and this year was no different.

Cindy blinked a few times to wake herself up. She rolled onto her side and looked out the small bedroom window.

Funny, I have never really looked out this window before, Cindy noted. *Has it always been here?*

Of course, it has! What a ridiculous question!

Cindy's head tilted. It was a usual insult, but there was less sting to the words today. It just fell flat.

Interesting.

She rolled onto her back and closed her eyes. She wasn't tired enough to go back to sleep, but her body felt like she had been in a punching match. Stiff and sore. She felt completely depleted.

You have work today.

I could call in sick.

But you aren't sick, so that would make you a liar.

Again, no sting.

I am tired, too tired to work.

But tired is not sick. Go to work!

There was a finality to the words that made Cindy sit up almost instantly.

Wait, she paused, *Father God, I don't know what to do in this situation. My body is telling me one thing, but my mind is saying another. I think this happens all of the time, but I am used to listening to my mind and silencing my body. What should I do?*

The room was quiet. After waiting a minute or two, Cindy sighed and started to get out of bed. As soon as she stood, a sharp pain shot through her side knocking her back on the bed.

"Ouch," she whimpered.

She slowed her breathing while holding her side. After a few seconds, the sharp pain receded.

Is this my answer? She asked the Lord.

Well, you sure can't work like this!

Agreed, she responded to whatever part was stating the obvious.

"Thank you, Lord, for allowing me to be aware

of what my body needs," Cindy whispered as she picked up her phone to call her boss.

Mrs. Watson was not available, so Cindy left her a voice message. Missing work was one of her least favorite things to do. If she ever did have to miss, it had to be worth the pain of the guilt and shame she would feel the entire day. Typically, she would just sleep through the day to avoid feeling it, but today didn't feel like a sleepy kind of day. She needed to rest for sure, but not sleep. She didn't know what kind of day it would be and that made her nervous.

Her usual coffee and spot at the kitchen table didn't hold any appeal this morning. Cindy crawled back into bed and pulled her thick comforter up around her. She didn't like how she felt. She didn't like feeling it, but she knew she needed to.

As she closed her eyes and started to relax, her internal world began to come into focus. For years Cindy had blocked this world out. She learned from seeing Mary that this was normal and even needed for her to survive the terrible trauma of her childhood. It was easy to block it out. She didn't even have to think about it. But to heal, to truly heal, she needed to open herself up to the world inside, to the horrors and the treasures buried deep.

Not so deep anymore, a voice responded.

True, Cindy thought.

The soft cries of the baby began to come into focus.

We are scared.

I know, Cindy replied.

As images of little children began to fill her mind, she began to feel the things she had been avoiding. She cringed, but she didn't stop them from flowing.

Around her, Zral and Abel began to lift their voices a little louder.

Salih and Rabok were close.

"Be on guard," instructed Michael as each of the angelic guards began to feel the presence of the Lord fill the room. They knew something was shifting for Cindy, and they wanted to cooperate with what the Holy Spirit was doing.

Cindy could feel something swirling around her feet and moving up her legs. Her body tensed. She wanted nothing more than to open her eyes, get ready for work, and become someone different for the day. Become someone who worked in retail. Someone who didn't have trauma or bad memories. Someone who felt no pain and who never disappointed anyone.

Disappointment? That was a new thought.

It is too much, someone whimpered.

What is? Cindy asked.

Hope.

The word hung in the air, and the wispy smoke of darkness that had crept into her bedroom rose higher around Cindy.

Hope is keeping us alive, Cindy finally responded.

No, it is killing us. The voice was weak and clearly in pain.

Small black darts began to fly through Cindy's bedroom, but they were no match for the quick-acting warrior angels stationed around the room.

If we didn't hope, we wouldn't continue to try and fail. The voice was confident. *Hope is killing us.*

The smoke was now consuming Cindy.

Discouragement, fear, disappointment. All of the years of trying, working, and failing, were wrapping in and through her mind. She could feel herself sinking deeper and deeper.

Mostly, Cindy felt confused. She had lost all hope of getting better before she met Mary. Once she began to learn about her dissociation it changed everything. She had hope again. If someone understood what was happening to her, then there must be a cure!

But we have tried everything, for so long.

Nothing works, nothing helps.

Nothing will ever change.

Cindy could feel the pain of despair. The pain of hopelessness. All the years gone…

The intensity of the battle was picking up pace in her room. The team could handle it, but the darkness being revealed was old and strong.

Without thinking, Cindy picked up a pen and the notepad she had purchased a few days ago and placed beside her bed.

She began to write:

> The pain was all around me,
> But I didn't know.
> The weight of it was hidden,
> Which allowed it to grow.
>
> One day it all became too much.
> Sorrow, pain, and grief.
> So, I looked where it was buried,
> In hopes for some relief.
>
> The grave was deeper and wider.
> Than I had ever known.
> But somehow, I felt connected
> To the pain seeds that had been sown.
>
> I wanted to escape the pain,
> But knowing it was mine,
> I could not give it up,
> It would be mine for all of time.

Fear struck me that it would be taken!
I must bury it even more.
But as I tried to hide it
My arms became tired and sore.

Cindy stopped, with her eyes frozen to the page.

Am I afraid to let the pain go?
All I ever wanted was to be free of the pain?
Is it?
Fear began to overtake her.

"This is all my fault! I will never be free! I don't even want to be free!" She exclaimed.

She could feel the tears starting to build. A lump was in her throat. She squeezed her eyes closed, now determined to shut it all down, but it was too late. A river was building internally, the smoke was rising externally, and a new voice was emerging from her heart. It was the voice in her heart that had seen it all. It had seen her pain, her struggle, her denial. The voice was raw and true, and she could not turn away from it.

She continued to write:

I noticed it was part of me.
And now out in the light,

It could not be hidden or removed.
No, that would not be right.

What will I do with my pain,
With my sorrow and the ache
Of all my life's story
Whatever could I make?

"Jesus," Cindy uttered.

She could feel the pain now more than she had ever felt it before. Tears rolled down her face, and her nose began to run. The lump in her throat grew as a painful weight settled in her chest.

As Cindy's cry reached the heart of God, the army surrounding her began to feel the strength of the Lord renew them. Their battle was not just with the evil surrounding Cindy, but it was with the ancient darkness that had held her entire family line throughout the generations. As each group of darkness in the room was defeated another would appear.

"God, please help me," Cindy cried again as she clutched her pen.

As Cindy's faith turned to the Lord, the swords around the room began to glow and the battle intensified.

Sobs of sorrow, anger, and pain flowed freely. It

felt like an eternity of pain was being released at that moment. Tears were streaming down Cindy's face, and she could hear her own cries of pain echo in her bedroom. They felt distant and detached, but she knew it was her own voice.

The smoke had completely consumed her now, and she let it. There was no more fight, no more strength, just surrender. This was her story. This was her pain.

If there was a God, and if this healing was going to happen, He would have to do it. She could not do anymore.

As she felt the stabbing pain of the despair and disappointment of a life of abuse and failures, something caught her eye. In the distance, beyond the cloud of smoke consuming her, she could see a light. She wasn't sure if the light was in her bedroom or in her mind's eye, but she knew it was real. The light was building in intensity. She took every ounce of her remaining strength and tried to focus on the light. It felt warm. It was drawing her.

She began to write again:

As the brightness of my Abba
Illuminated the hurt.
I saw that it was all changing.
And there was no more dirt.

Each piece showed signs of wear,
But it no longer looked so worn.
Each piece was now much stronger.
They could not be torn.

Somehow without me knowing.
My Heavenly Father above,
Had taken all the remnants.
And bathed them with His love.

Now my pain was different,
It was stronger, bolder, clean.
Now my pain was healing.
And there was strength was underneath.

As I breathed in the air around me
I knew that I had changed.
My loving Heavenly Father
Was taking all my shame.

The smoke was changing as Cindy wrote. She thought the smoke was something evil, something meant to kill her, but it wasn't.

She watched in amazement as the smoke began to take the shape of little children. Some were sad, some were angry, and some were crying and withdrawn. The smoke was gone, and now the room in her mind was filled with children who had carried the shame of her abuse, the shame of her abusers, and the shame she had taken on as her own over the years. She began to realize that her fear of disappointment was really her shame. Shame that she was never good enough. Shame of her failures and insecurities. Shame in her very identity and existence.

As the light of the Lord transformed the smoke into pieces of her heart, she noticed the shame was not really hers. The word "failure" hung in the air. It was no longer rooted to these children, these parts of her heart. She didn't know what it was now or what it meant, but she knew it was changing. She looked back to the children and saw herself for the first time.

> I thought my pain was ugly,
> So, I resisted it being seen.
> But now I can see clearly,
> My pain is part of me.
>
> The shame made me feel ugly.
> It was shame that made the pain look bad.
> I couldn't see it for all these years.
> Shame was rooted behind the sad.

The shame is gone.
My pain has changed.
And now I am so strong.
My Father did this for me
To Him, I do belong.

Belonging. It was what she had always wanted. She had never really belonged anywhere. She tilted her head as another thought occurred to her.

The pain, I have always belonged to the pain. Fresh tears rolled down her face.

I accept my pain as my own, Cindy thought. *I can now that I see the shame.*

I don't want to belong to the pain, a little voice went through her mind.

As quick as the thought landed in her heart, another statement followed.

"You are Mine, lovely daughter." The words were strong but filled with the kindness of a loving Heavenly Father.

More tears.

"You have always been Mine." The love of her Heavenly Father began to fill her heart and mind as she wept.

Throughout her room and the entire home, light filled the space. The angelic guards were no longer fighting, they didn't have to. The Light singed every bit of darkness in every nook and cranny of the home. The song of the worshippers could be heard for blocks.

"Glory to the King of Kings,
Glory to the Lord,
Glory to the Word of God,
There is power in His Sword!"

As each of the little children in Cindy's heart was transformed into their truest selves, clean and healed of their pain, Cindy's heart filled with gratitude. She continued to write.

Thank you, Heavenly Father
For showing me the truth
Thank you for my healing!
And getting to the root.

My story's being written.
Still from day to day.
You promised you'll complete it.
In Your own special way.

Make me in Your image.
With Your heart, Your strength, Your peace

And fill me with Your Spirit
So, all my shame will cease.

Then I will be stronger
Than I've ever been before.
And I will keep on growing,
In the image of my Lord.

The last two lines she wrote hung in the air: And I will keep on growing, in the image of my Lord.

The image of my Lord.

What does this mean? She wondered.

We can't be made in God's image. We are. . .

The voice stopped. As each part of her began to look around, they realized they were not covered in dirt and grime anymore. They had changed. They were clean.

The smoke of despair and disappointment was used to hide their shame, but the shame was never theirs to begin with. The word GRACE appeared in Cindy's mind. The letters were written in the shape of a cross. This symbol was often triggering to her, but today it held a new meaning. The shape was not the focus, the GRACE was. God's grace had redeemed her. She didn't need to hide the shame, because the grace of God had cleansed the shame away.

A new sense of peace washed over her. She felt a few tears wash down her face as she drifted off to sleep.

As she rested, Michael and the guard worshipped and praised the Lord for the mighty victory they had just witnessed.

Chapter 5

"This is unacceptable!" Darlene did not raise her voice to the nervous banker, but if looks could scream, she was at full volume. "My husband and I have been customers here for more than forty years. There is no need for the additional hassle." She stood with her feet firmly planted at the teller's counter. Her jaw was set. She was not moving until her situation was resolved.

"I am so sorry, ma'am, it is simply the bank's policy that two people are needed to open the. . ."

"I will not speak to you further. Where is your manager?"

The teller knew better than to utter another word. He silently rose and disappeared into the back office.

Business continued around the small bank office. Customers scurried in and out trying to complete their business without making eye contact or being noticed by the angry woman. Tellers did their best to stay focused on their own customers for fear she might engage them. After a few minutes, a young woman appeared from the back of the office.

"Can I help you, ma'am?" She inquired with a polite smile.

"I should hope so! I would like to open my lockbox, and this teller told me it was not possible." She shot a glare at the teller who was now helping another customer. "The contents of that lockbox belong to me, and I demand you let me have them."

"I understand. The contents of the lockbox do belong to you, and I assure you that no one has access to those contents, but you and your husband." The manager paused, "unfortunately, you signed a contract that stated it could only be opened if both of you were present." The manager quietly slid a copy of the contract across the counter while maintaining eye contact with her angry customer.

"Well, I never!" Darlene tilted her face and glared at the woman as if to break her will simply through mental power. The manager just stood there, relaxed and with one hand on the corner of the contract. After a moment the awkward standoff ended, and Darlene stormed out of the bank. Behind her swirled angry demons spewing insults and curses at everyone and everything.

As Darlene's SUV pulled onto the long driveway to her farmhouse, her anger was building to a point of no return. "That stupid, stupid man! Why would he make me sign that contract keeping me out of my own lockbox? He will pay for this!"

She burst into the house looking for her husband Derek. "Derek!" Her voice echoed through the vaulted entry and throughout the house.

No answer.

As she stormed through the kitchen slamming cabinets and cursing at the air, the black from the yard began oozing through the bottom of the walls into the home. Her anger was fueled by the toxic evil polluting the farmhouse property. There was nothing to stop it. No one to even notice it.

"Ding dong," the sound interrupted her rant. She waited for a moment to see if her husband would get it. The pause in her tantrum gave her a moment to remember that Derek had a business meeting today and was not home.

"Hmph," she slammed one more door and straightened her blouse before heading to the front of the house. She made it just as the guest was ringing the bell a second time.

As she opened the door, a wave of light burst through the darkness that was simmering around her knees pushing it back to the edges of the elegant foyer. "Can I help you?" Darlene inquired of the middle–aged man standing at the door.

"Yes, actually," he smiled politely. "My name is Reverend Jacobs. I am from the church down the road."

Darlene tried to smile politely, but she could hear the murmurs of anger and complaints all around her. She could feel the pressure building in the room. "I am aware of it, but my husband and I attend church already, and we are not interested in changing." She went to shut the door, but the man continued.

"Excellent!" He smiled warmly, "I'm glad you and your husband have a church home. I am actually here on a different matter."

Darlene paused halfway through slamming the door and raised an eyebrow indicating he could continue.

The darkness was pushing back on the light that was now flooding the entryway. "Well, a few weeks ago, the school down the road flooded. They have been working hard to repair the damage but have run out of money."

"Of course," Darlene muttered under her breath.

The minister continued, "we are reaching out to a few of the county neighbors to see if we can raise money to help them finish the work so the kids can get back to school."

Darlene opened her mouth to tell the man they were unable to help when she stopped for a moment. The light was strong, stronger than the darkness. The Holy Spirit was calling, inviting her to engage with holiness even for just a moment, and she could feel it.

"I'm not sure," she started. "I will have to talk with my husband."

"Here is my card," he handed her a business card. "Feel free to give me a call anytime."

She took the card and just stared at it. The door closed and she just stood there, looking at the card. She felt something, but she didn't know what. There was something small and still happening around her. She could almost hear it. She put the card on the entry table and walked into the living room. The darkness filled the space as the light seeped out of the house.

Chapter 6

Cindy rolled over and yawned. It was Thursday, session day.

The week had crawled by, not in a bad way though.

I guess this is what happens when I don't lose time, she thought to herself.

She had some time before her late morning session, so she decided to take a drive.

Michael led the troops through the usual checks and routines that went along with Cindy's drives. "She hasn't made a habit of taking drives like this until recently," Michael commented to Gabe, "It seems there is always a purpose to it though."

"She seems more restful this week," Gabe observed as Cindy climbed into her little Toyota and started the engine.

"She is," Rabok responded.

"We have not seen her feel so much of her own heart before," Salih joined in the conversation.

"The more she feels, the easier it is for her to function and to rest." Both Salih and Rabok seemed pleased with their charge's newfound state of mind.

"This is true, but it also brings so much of her past to the surface, that it can easily bring in confusion too," Michael cautioned.

"Why?" Gabe wondered.

"As she functions and rests better, she assumes she is improving - which she is," Michael paused to choose his words. "But a big aspect of improving means remembering and feeling painful things."

"I see," Gabe was beginning to understand.

"So, it can be very confusing when improvement feels like a setback."

Gabe nodded. Ever since he began learning about God's design for coping with childhood trauma, he had been fascinated and overwhelmed. It was good to learn, but also difficult to reconcile how it all worked. Progress with some confusion.

"I think I know how she feels," he said to himself.

Before Cindy could get out of the driveway, she received a text from Mary.

"I'm so sorry, but I need to cancel our session today. I will let you know if I can do a makeup session in the next few days."

Cindy's heart sank. She needed that session. She

needed every session. One week was hard enough to get through, could she make it through two? She shifted the car into reverse and backed out of the drive. She pushed the thoughts of disappointment and sadness aside and shifted into drive.

"That was a blow," Salih commented.

"It was, but she recovered well," Michael noted.

"Nothing evil tried to take advantage," Hezek reported.

"Praise be to the Most High God," they all declared.

Cindy was now driving at a steady speed out of town and into the country. Her window was down, and the wind was whipping her hair around.

"It can be confusing to experience so much healing, be able to rest for the first time in your life, and also be struggling with such deep pain that you doubt your ability to continue to go on," Michael explained.

"I see," Gabe was beginning to understand more about Cindy and her journey.

Cindy was in the country now. Trees and wooden fences lined the road. Cattle, old barns, and rustic farmhouses littered the fields, while giant solar windmills lined the horizon. It was home. She had known this countryside for her entire life. Of course, when she was little, the giant windmills weren't there, but most of the rest were.

Why am I here? What am I doing?

Cindy's mind was still relatively quiet, but she could feel them. The parts of her heart that broke off when the trauma became too much for her. She could only imagine what it was like as a child, suffering the way they did. The way she did.

No.

This line of thinking is not allowed, someone told her.

I know, was all she said.

Her mind cleared of all thoughts, and she just drove. She drove until it was dark, and then she kept driving.

Michael and the troops were with her. The Spirit of God was with her. Her parts were all with her, but she felt none of them. It was just her and the road.

Around 1:00 am, her eyes became so heavy she knew she needed to pull over. She was just entering the edge of Smithton, a mid-sized midwestern town in the middle of nowhere in particular. It didn't take long for her to find a hotel and get checked in.

I hate hotels.

I know.

I'm so tired.

Michael had already dispatched his troops to check the space in and around the hotel and received an "all clear." There were the usual suspects of evil here and there, but none seemed to care much about Cindy or the angelic guard, and none were in or around her room.

As Cindy entered the newly renovated hotel room, she turned all the lights on and checked the bathroom and the closet. The room was nicely furnished and smelled as if it had been recently cleaned. There were six pillows on the bed and the comforter was plush and cool. She sat on the edge of the bed and kicked her shoes off. Her eyes were burning now.

She laid back on the pillows and closed her eyes. Sleep overtook her.

Zral and Abel sang songs of thanks to the Most High God while Rabok and Salih sat with Cindy.

Kaleb and Hezek stood to watch. No other warriors were needed. The space was clean and clear.

Before long, the presence of the Lord began to settle on the small hotel room. In response, Michael and the others joined Zral and Abel in their worship of the Most High God.

Around 4:00 am, Cindy stumbled into the bathroom, got a drink of water, and then snuggled into the king-size bed this time under the warmth of the down comforter. Sleep came easily. Worship continued throughout the night.

As the sun rose in the distance, Cindy remained fast asleep.

"The Holy Spirit is working," Rabok told the others.

Michael turned his attention to Rabok and Salih who were close to Cindy's side.

"Yes," agreed Salih. "I sense His presence as well, and I can feel her heart open to the Lord."

"The dreams are changing," Michael observed with a smile.

"What are they changing to?" Gabe asked.

"I don't know, but if the Lord is doing it, then it is good."

Ten o'clock came and Cindy awoke to her phone ringing on the nightstand. She rolled over without opening her eyes and pushed the button on the side to silence the sound. As she pulled a pillow close to her side and snuggled into the soft bed, she took a deep breath and turned her attention to the Lord.

"Thank you, God. Thank you for getting me here safely. Thank you for good sleep. Thank you for," she paused. "I don't really know what you are doing, God. I want to thank you for healing, but I don't even know if that is happening."

She rolled onto her back and pulled the pillow over her stomach.

With her eyes still closed, she continued to talk to the Lord. "Truthfully, I don't ever really know what is happening. I just feel like I am blindly doing this tug-of-war thing with life," she tilted her head as she looked up, "with you."

She closed her eyes again. "I guess what I am saying is," Cindy searched for the words that matched the feeling in her heart. "I guess I want what you want. What you want for me. I don't know exactly if that is even possible – I feel pretty far gone – but it's what I want."

The swords started to glow around the room, as the presence of the Holy Spirit soaked into the room again.

"I surrender my heart and mind to you. I don't want to fight you anymore. Please help me to not fight you anymore." As her shoulders began to relax, she realized how much tension she had been carrying.

I feel so different, she thought.

Then she laughed, *how many times I am going to feel "different." I don't even know what that means anymore.*

With a smile on her face, she took a quick shower and then checked out of the hotel.

This was a nice stay. I'll have to remember it. She put her home address in the GPS.

Five hours later she arrived back home.

You would think that would have taken longer given how long I drove yesterday, she thought. *I must have been driving in circles most of the day.*

"Gotta love those country roads!" She said out loud as she climbed out of the car.

Thankfully, she was off work today, so she decided to do a little more writing. She opened her journal and flipped to the first open page. The end of the poem she had written a few nights before caught her eye:

Make me in Your image.
With Your heart, Your strength, Your peace
And fill me with Your Spirit
So, all my shame will cease.

Then I will be stronger
Than I've ever been before.
And I will keep on growing,
In the image of my Lord.

She remembered how powerful it was when she wrote it. It was like she was writing it with the Holy Spirit. It was theirs together.

Is it even possible for all my shame to cease? Can I ever truly be what God created me to be? She wondered.

Not after everything.

She could feel the old familiar shame creeping to the surface. She didn't want to feel it. The peace over the past 12 hours was not enough. She wanted it longer.

Angela, I'll call Angela.

Angela had a way of calming her soul. *Lord, please help her be available.*

"Is she going to spiral?" Hezek asked with his hand on his sword.

"I don't think so," Michael was smiling. "She is choosing hope. I think she will be ok."

"Hello?" Angela answered her phone after just one ring.

Cindy froze for a moment, and then she heard her own voice speaking into the phone.

"Hi Angela, it's Cindy."

"Hi, Cindy! It's good to hear from you." Cindy could feel Angela's pleasant smile on the phone.

"I was wondering if you were available for coffee?"

That was too direct.

You didn't even ask how she was first.

Or if she was busy.

Cindy focused her attention on the phone and tried to ignore her inner doubts and shame.

"Sure! Let me drop my daughter off for her dance class, and I can meet you at our usual spot."

Usual spot. Wow, when did we get a usual spot?

"Um," Cindy focused back on the call, "ok, 4:00?"

"Sounds good. See you then!"

Just like that Cindy had a coffee date!

I can't believe I just did that.

It was a mistake.

I don't want to be embarrassed.

The shame started to creep in.

"Jesus, I know this shame isn't mine anymore," she imagined dropping the shame with Jesus.

"I am a new creature in Christ." She didn't know where the verse came from as her mouth declared the words, but Michael did.

Cindy changed her clothes and headed to the coffee shop.

She arrived a little early but made her way inside anyway. The shop was almost empty. Two teens, maybe college students, sat in the corner working on a project together. A young mom with her toddler sat by the window putting a puzzle together. The familiar smell of coffee pastries hung in the air as soft music drifted from the speakers in the ceiling. Cindy ordered a coffee and a cherry cheesecake flip and sat at the table by the fireplace.

Waiting for Angela was easy at first, but then Cindy's mind began to fill with thoughts. It started with faint images of her abuse and abusers. Then pictures of embarrassing moments and poor decisions began to roll through her mind. She glanced at each one. There was only a small bit of emotion, but she couldn't identify what it was.

"Hi, Cindy!" Cindy was startled out of her mental slideshow by a kind and familiar voice.

"Hi, Angela," she felt herself blushing, but she wasn't sure why. "Thank you for meeting me."

They hugged as was their routine.

"I am going to grab a coffee. Be right back." Angela smiled again and then turned and headed to the counter.

Cindy watched her walk away. There was an ease about how she walked. It was peaceful and light.

Why does she bother with us? Someone wanted to know.

I really don't know.

She is so kind. Why does she listen to us?

Before Cindy could reply Angela was back with her coffee. "So how did sale week go?" Angela asked with a smile.

"Whew!" Cindy feigned exhaustion, "it was rough!"

Angela laughed her simple laugh.

"It was good though."

"I'm glad. They always have such great deals, but

I can't imagine what it would be like to work there. It can get really busy over that week."

"It was busy," Cindy took a drink of her coffee.

Okay, so we are here. Now what?

She didn't know.

"It was good to see you at church last week. I'm sorry I didn't get a chance to say hi."

"That's ok, I had to leave right after service."

"What did you think of the new late service?" Angela asked casually.

"It was good."

You are killing it here.

Shut up, this is all new.

You have to say something, anything. You are just acting like a lump on a log.

"Lump on a log," the words echoed through Cindy's mind and accidentally slipped out of her mouth.

"Excuse me?" Angela asked. "I didn't quite hear you."

"Lump on a log. Funny, I haven't thought about that in years." Cindy was still muttering.

"Lump on a log?" Angela asked again.

"Yes," Cindy jerked from the images in her head and focused back on Angela. "My mom used to call me that when I was little."

Angela crossed her arms on the table and leaned

in a bit, the way she did when she was ready to listen to Cindy talk.

"You don't talk about your parents very much," Angela commented.

"I know," Cindy looked away for a moment. "When I was little, we went to a lot of social events. Some for church, others for social clubs and, I don't know, just different things." Cindy tried to take a deep breath but noticed her abdomen felt restrained a bit. She continued. "Sometimes I just didn't feel like participating. I didn't want to be pretty or shown off. I didn't want to talk to every boring adult that came around."

Cindy was surprised as the words came from her mouth.

"My mom would call me a 'lump on a log' in front of everyone. They would all laugh like it was a good joke." Cindy's voice cracked as she spoke. "But I knew it meant I was in trouble. The kind of trouble that..." Her voice trailed off.

After a moment of silence, Angela replied. "Being a kid can be hard."

She has no idea.

"Yeah," Cindy wiped a tear. "I have really been wrestling with this question, it kind of relates."

Are we seriously still talking?

Cindy pushed the internal voices aside.

"What is it?"

"Well, I don't understand how God can take someone who has lived an awful and shameful life and make it like those things, those choices, didn't happen."

"What do you mean?"

"I mean, how does it take it all away so someone can be 'new in Christ'?" Cindy knew the question was too big for a coffee date. Plus, she must sound like an awful person asking it.

"That's a good question," Angela took a moment to think it over as she took another drink of her coffee. "I don't know exactly how He does it, but I know that He does."

"Oh," was all Cindy could say.

"I know he doesn't take away our past," Angela began. "What has happened, has happened. But it's like," she paused again to choose her words. "It's like nothing can happen that is too big for God to work with. He can take any awful thing and make it into something new. I think that is what Romans 8:28 is about when it says, 'He works all things together for our good.'"

"I know, it just seems more complicated than that," Cindy replied.

"I agree."

Before Angela could say more, they were

interrupted by another familiar voice.

"Well, hi there!"

Red scarf man!

Cindy turned to see Daniel approaching their table.

"Hi, Angela! It is good to see you." His smile was big and warm. Angela stood and gave him a hug.

"I know you," Daniel started as he looked at Cindy. His smile was warm, and his eyes were kind.

She looked down nervously. She did not want another big bear hug, so she decided to stay firmly planted in her seat. "Hi," she responded weakly.

"You work at the store downtown!"

She was surprised he remembered.

"Yes, I do," she gave a slight smile.

"It was a nice surprise to see you at church on Sunday. I am so new to town; it was good to see a familiar face." He gave her a playful wink and patted her on the shoulder.

There it was again!

Did I just see the kindness of Jesus in his eyes?

"Well, I will let you two get back to your coffee," he said as he began to walk away.

"I should be in the office first thing Monday to start planning our summer calendar," Angela told him.

"Sounds good. I will see you then. Goodbye,

ladies!"

He went to the counter and picked up his call-ahead coffee order and was out the door in a flash.

"So, I see you have met our new Connections Pastor?" Angela asked.

Cindy was thankful to be off the topic of her past and her mother, so she embraced the new topic thankfully.

"Yes, I have. He seems nice."

"He is. My husband and I have known him for years since college. We were so excited when he was able to come on as a pastor here!"

"That is pretty great," Cindy didn't know what to say.

"Oh, dear!" Angela exclaimed as she glanced at her phone. "The time has gotten away from me! I need to run, but I am really glad you called." She gave Cindy another warm smile as she stood and gathered her things. "See you Sunday?"

"Sure," Cindy regretted answering that way, but it was too late.

"Bye!

"Bye."

Cindy's shoulders slumped as Angela hurried out of the coffee shop. She thought of the peace and light that both Daniel and Angela brought to a room, and she didn't know how she could ever have that. She did feel like a lump on a log. Just a big, awkward, difficult, lump on a log.

A tinge of shame came over her as she realized she was repeating her mom's words. She pushed it aside and headed out of the coffee shop to her car.

"Life sure feels like a roller coaster," she said as she turned the car on and headed home.

Chapter 7

Darlene and Derek were sitting at the dinner table. The sun was still bright as its rays shone through the large picture window. To see this room in the natural, it had all the elegance and demure of a well-loved estate. To see it in the spirit was an entirely different thing. Strings of black goo were draped around the tall candlesticks in the corner and over the large mirror. The table looked like a massive food fight had occurred – years ago, and never been cleaned. Tar and thick oil were still seeping through the walls into the interior of the home.

Perhaps the saddest of all was the state of Darlene and Derek. Darlene was bound by a thick, worn leather jacket. Instead of the years making it worn and weak, it had become worn and hardened. The same thick oil dripping into the house coated the evil coat making it difficult to get near without being slimed.

Derek did not appear bound. In fact, at first glance, he looked perfectly fine. His posture was perfect, and his dress shirt and slacks were pristine. Upon further inspection, a shackle could be seen on his left ankle. The shackle left bruises and cuts where it had rubbed and pinched throughout the decades. Attached to the shackle was a thick, tar-covered chain that led to a tall, evil entity not four feet away. The chain was taught, with no room for movement without permission from the large beast.

This home was far from elegant and free. It was a prison. It was filled with darkness and ruled by evil. An evil that Derek had chosen for their family decades ago. This evil consumed them both, and although God had made opportunities for their freedom, neither of them had made any moves to gain that freedom. As the couple ate their breakfast in silence, their own thoughts of jealousy, pride, and shame filled their hearts.

Darlene was the first to speak. "I went to the bank earlier this week."

Derek didn't look up.

"I thought I would get that beautiful pendant out of the lockbox – you know, the one my mother gave me, and wear it to the inauguration at the ladies club later this month."

Still, no response from Derek, but a small vein began to pulse in his neck. He slowly took another bite of his steak.

"Well, strange thing," Darlene said, as she could feel the tension building in the room, but she continued anyway. "It seems there must be two people there to unlock the box." She paused, but still Derek did not respond. "Were you aware of that?"

The silence hung in the air like a threat. Darlene was all too familiar with this threat, and she feared she had taken things too far.

Derek laid his fork down beside his plate. The chain to the beast guarding him gave a slight yank and Derek's fists closed and tightened. "Do not lie to me," he stated in his normal tone, but with an edge of hate. "I know what you were really there for." He still did not look up from his plate. The vein in his neck was now protruding and Darlene knew she had to come clean and beg for mercy.

"I was thinking of the pendant," she searched for the least incriminating words possible, "but truthfully, I was also thinking of the certificates we have from your grandfather," she paused to check Derek's response. No change. "I mean, they are worth a lot of money, and they could get us out of this trouble with the man that holds the deed to our house."

Her husband hit the table with his fist as the chain yanked one more time. He slowly stood and somehow appeared to be ten feet tall as he yelled at his wife. "I told you I would handle it! Those certificates are not to be touched under any circumstances! Do I make myself clear?"

Darlene was trembling, but she held her head high and replied, "Yes, sir."

She waited as he stormed out of the room and out of the house. As soon as she heard his car engine start, she crumbled into a ball of tears of anger and resentment on the table. Her heart hurt, her chest hurt, her head hurt. How long could she keep this up? She was living with a madman controlled by his evil desires, and all she wanted was to be free.

"Are you done, ma'am?" The cook had entered the dining room to clear the table.

Darlene quickly gathered her composure, sat up, and responded with hate in her voice. "Of course, we are done! We were done ten minutes ago! You should have these dishes washed and cleaned by now. What is wrong with you!" With that, she shoved her chair back and stomped out of the dining room.

As she passed through the foyer and headed to the spiral staircase, the business card from Pastor Jacobs caught her eye.

"I thought I threw that away," she mumbled.

As she picked it up, a tiny beam of light cut through the darkness around her and poked through the leather bondage of shame and hate holding her hostage. She grabbed her phone and dialed the number.

"Pastor Jacobs?" she inquired as a man's voice answered the phone.

"Yes, this is him," was the response. "What can I do for you?"

"I think it is more what I can do for you," she said with authority in her voice. "This is Darlene, you came to my house a few days ago?"

"Oh yes, it is good to hear from you," he replied.

"Well, it turns out I do have a little time, and I would love to know what more I can do for that poor school." She tried to sound sincere, stuffing all the angst deep inside.

"Excellent!"

"Would it be possible to come to take a tour of the school tomorrow just so I can better understand the situation?"

"Sure! Tomorrow is Saturday, but I will be at the office to unlock the building for the teens. They are having a big event this weekend."

She didn't care. *Will you be there or not?*

"So," he continued. "I will be at the office around 9:00 am. Stop by any time in the morning and we will head over."

"That would be fine. Thank you, sir." She hung up the phone without waiting for a reply.

The evening and night came and went with no words spoken between the bitter and angry couple.

Saturday morning finally arrived, and there was still an odd silence at the old farmhouse. This silence was not only apparent in the home, but across the entire property. Typically, the birds were singing, and the wind could be heard blowing through the treetops. Spring was in full bloom, and that was Darlene's favorite time of the year. It seemed like anything could be possible.

Years ago, Darlene would spend weeks planning and redecorating the house. She would have a dozen gardeners come to freshen up the landscaping and plant new flowers. Some years, she would even throw out her entire wardrobe and buy a new one. Spring was a time of fresh starts, and that was what she needed today.

She was careful not to wake her husband as she changed and headed downstairs for breakfast. Something quick to eat would be good, and then she would head to the church. Of course, it was early, so maybe she would drive down her favorite spring lane on the way.

As she gathered her purse and keys, she headed to the garage. Derek had bought her the car of her dreams three years ago. It was an anniversary gift, one of the few she truly cherished.

She remembered driving around town as a child in her mom's Cadillac. She felt so safe and secure back then. In fact, she had married Derek in hopes of finding that same feeling of safety and security, and she did, for a while. But soon life turned, as it often does, and she was left feeling empty and hopeless.

I think that's why spring is so important to me, she thought. *It's a chance to start over.*

Unfortunately, no matter how much redecorating, relandscaping, and retooling of her life she did, things were still the same, and nowadays they seemed to be getting worse.

She climbed into the beautiful blue Cadillac and shut the car door. Her dream car now felt like a tomb instead of freedom.

The drive to the church was only fifteen minutes from her home, but it was only 8:00 a.m., so she decided to take the long way.

About ten years ago, Darlene discovered this

road. She called it "Azalea Pathway." Azaleas of all kinds lined the road on either side. The bushes were framed by a pristine white picket fence that outlined the property of the Millers. Their family had lived on these acres for longer than anyone knew. Bright purple eastern redbuds and delicate white dogwood trees littered the fields behind the azaleas. A few pine trees were in the mix as well. The colors were vibrant and alive against the deep green grass and beautiful blue sky.

Darlene drove slowly down the road. There were no other cars in sight. She wanted to take in the beauty and breathe the fresh spring air. It felt so different than what she had ever known. The Millers seemed to have everything she ever wanted. They weren't as wealthy or prominent as Darlene and her husband, but still, there was something about them. And there was definitely something about this property.

As Darlene excited Azalea Pathway, she picked up speed and redirected her thinking to the church and the flooded school.

They need to take better care of that school. I'm sure it's their own fault it was flooded to begin with.

Her thoughts were filled with judgments and complaints about the city, the government, and the world in general. When she finally arrived at the church, the life of Azalea Pathway was gone, and her invisible leather jacket hugged her just as tight as usual.

"Good morning!" Pastor Jacobs greeted Darlene as soon as she walked in the door.

"Good morning," she responded with a polite, but stiff smile.

They shook hands, and she followed him into his office.

"My wife is here today helping out with the teens," he started, "she hasn't been to the school in several months and was interested in seeing their progress as well."

"Good to see you again, Darlene," Mrs. Jacobs started. "I believe we met a few years back at my bakery in town."

Mrs. Amy Jacobs. Darlene remembered her. She never liked her. She was just too happy all of the time.

No one could be that happy. Darlene thought.

"Nice to see you again as well," Darlene played the part.

They all sat in the office. Darlene wasn't sure why. Shouldn't they be headed to the school?

Pastor Jacobs picked up the phone and made a call while Mrs. Jacobs made small talk with Darlene.

"So have you lived in the area for quite a long

time?" she inquired.

"Yes, my husband, Derek, grew up here. I moved here when we married, let's see, that was 40 years ago."

"Funny how time goes by."

Funny how we aren't doing what I came here to do, Darlene thought.

Pastor Jacobs hung up the phone. "The principal is headed to the school to show us around. She should be there in 30 minutes or so."

"That would be fine," Darlene responded.

"We will head that way in 15 minutes or so," he added.

"Can I get you a bottle of water or a cup of coffee?" Mrs. Jacobs asked.

"No, thank you," Darlene was polite, but wearing thin. It had been years since she had been out in the community. Most of her social engagements were at her home, in her own space, with her rules. This felt uncomfortable.

Darlene decided to push into the small talk to make the time go by a little quicker. "You have a beautiful family," she said, pointing to a picture of Pastor Jacobs, his wife, and their two children.

"Why, thank you!" Mrs. Jacobs responded. "That's an old picture. Kaitlin and Billy are both in college now," she stared off toward something invisible just past the picture. "They grow so fast."

"Indeed, they do," Darlene agreed.

"Do you have any children?" the pastor asked.

"A daughter," Darlene responded. "If it's ok, can we head over to the school now? I don't mind waiting a few minutes in the parking lot."

Mrs. Jacobs was a little caught off guard but adjusted quickly. "That would be fine." She turned to her husband, "I will check on the youth leader and his group, and then we can head over."

Pastor Jacobs nodded in agreement and the three split ways.

Darlene was happy to be back in her car, her space, and her rules. She didn't know when social interactions became so overwhelming to her. She wanted the life she had always dreamed of. She used to love dinner parties, visiting with friends, and traveling all over the country. For a while, she thought she had the life she always wanted, but it turned out it was all a sham. It all felt so empty.

Darlene turned onto the road to the school. Construction trucks and a smattering of tools and building materials were in the parking lot. The building looked fine from the outside, maybe a little worn, but fine. Her blue Cadillac turned into the bus parking lane and stopped next to the curb. After a few minutes, the Jacobs pulled in behind her, and they were quickly joined by a lady dressed casually with a large set of keys in hand.

Darlene took a deep breath and got out of the car.

"Hello," she said as she approached the trio.

"This is Darlene. She and her husband live outside of town." Mrs. Jacobs introduced Darlene to the woman with the keys.

The woman held out her hand and introduced herself as they shook hands. "I am Mrs. Batter, the school principal. I'd be happy to show you around the school."

Darlene nodded in agreement, and the four headed into the building.

The tour was long, and the principal gave way more information than Darlene needed or wanted.

As they approached their vehicles outside, Darlene realized she was feeling more worn and tired than she could handle. "Thank you so much for your time, Mrs. Batter, and Mr. and Mrs. Jacobs. You have given me a lot to think about." Pastor Jacobs started to speak, but Darlene raised her hand to stop him and continued to speak. "I will speak with my husband, and we will get back to you." With that, she was back in her car and headed home.

Her heart hurt. She didn't know why. She didn't know what she needed. She knew whatever it was, she didn't have it. Tears ran down her face as she turned down the long driveway that led to her farmhouse.

Chapter 8

It was Saturday evening and Cindy was driving home from work. Saturdays used to be Cindy's favorite day. She loved to be off work and visit with friends and do fun things.

Fun things, I don't even know what that is anymore.

She truly didn't. She couldn't remember what she used to do for fun or how she would spend her Saturdays. Now Saturday was just another day to get through.

When did that change? She wondered.

Five years ago.

Oh yes, five years ago. When the memories got worse, the pain started breaking through to the surface.

I want to enjoy life again; she thought as she drove home from work. *I want to know what it's like to live, not just to survive.*

Is that even possible?

No, it's not.

I want to go home.

Home? What home? Cindy drove quietly to her house.

The past two days had been smooth. That surprised her, given counseling for the week was canceled. Mary had sent another text saying they would not meet until next Thursday, but somehow it was okay. Cindy knew she would be okay. She parked in front of her house and closed her eyes.

"God, thank you for all your help. I don't want to be ungrateful, but I want to experience life again. I want to like something, maybe even love something again. I don't even know if I ever have." She thought for a moment but didn't know what else to say. As she climbed out of the car, she felt the all too familiar feeling of shame wash over her.

We don't deserve good things.

Too much bad has happened.

It can't be erased.

It can't be undone.

Cindy struggled to get inside the house under the weight of her story. As the memories had been slowly returning, the reality of her life story was sinking in. She dropped her keys and purse just inside the door and headed into the living room.

Kaleb stood ahead of her, alert and ready for what might happen next. "The shame seems to be getting stronger," he commented.

"No," Michael corrected, "it is simply coming to the surface. Shame was at the deepest root of Cindy's trauma. God dealt with the spirit of shame a few days ago, but now Cindy is working through the impact it has had on her life."

"Shame? How can that be?" Gabe asked. "The trauma wasn't her doing. She isn't to blame."

"That doesn't matter." Michael's face was sober as he continued. "She was so young, and the trauma was too intense. She took on the shame of the acts of abuse. The shame of her abusers became her own."

"That is unbelievable," Gabe was stunned at the thought that someone so innocent could have been forced to take the blame for acts that were so evil.

"It was the only way she could make sense of what was happening to her," Michael continued.

"If it was her fault, her shame, then somehow it made sense," Salih started. "If it was the shame of the abusers then it felt as if the world was completely out of her control. This is one of the scariest feelings for children. They have an innate need to understand their place in the world and how things work. Violence like this does not create safety."

"Exactly," Michael agreed. "So, she took on the weight of evil. If it was her fault, if she was actually bad, then it would all make sense."

"That is incredible," Gabe shook his head at the thought. "Surely now as an adult, she knows it wasn't her fault?"

"Part of her does," Michael answered. "But she still battles shame. It impacts her identity, who she believes she is. Only God can show her the truth of who she is and who she was made to be."

Cindy was tired. It was early, and there was no real reason to go to bed, but she needed to. She needed to sleep.

Feeling things is hard.

It is exhausting.

The little one was crying again.

"Dear God," Cindy prayed, "I want to stay connected to my heart. I want to truly live each minute of my life. But it is so exhausting. Please help me." She drifted to sleep before she could finish her prayer.

Sunday morning came with more rain and dark, gloomy clouds. If it weren't for Cindy feeling obligated to Angela, she would not be going to church today.

Thank goodness for the new late service!

Amen.

A small smile crossed Cindy's face as the parts discussed going to church and singing the songs and doing the church thing. They seemed to be adjusting a bit to the changes that were happening. She didn't dare mention it though or it might scare them a bit.

You know we can hear you?

We are all here with your thoughts too!

Cindy laughed out loud.

"Busted!" she proclaimed as she poured her coffee.

While she drank her coffee and ate her eggs, she thought about what life might be like if the trauma hadn't happened. Who would she be? What would she be doing? She had never allowed these thoughts to be in her mind before. They were too painful.

Maybe then God would have given us a purpose.

Then we could be like the people at church or in the Bible.

Then we could be good!

Too much! Too much!

It was too much. Too much to think about and to hope for. Too much! She took her dishes to the sink and decided to watch outback to see if any bluebirds were visiting her birdhouse yet before heading to church.

A few small birds came and checked it out while

she was watching. She loved to watch the freedom of the birds. They could come and go as they pleased. They could get away from most any situation, and their voice was always happy. They were always singing. She had never heard a grumpy bird in her whole life.

She chuckled at the thought.

Suddenly, she realized she had lost all track of time and was almost late for church. She hurried to her room, changed quickly, and sped away in her little Toyota.

As she approached the parking lot at church, she smiled at all the traffic in and out. It was good the church was growing. It was good that people were finding God. She was so grateful to have this community, and she was even learning to navigate the parking lot between the two services! As she wove through the cars, she was able to park in her usual parking spot. It felt kind of good to be here.

Shocking! A voice mocked from inside.

Hush up, it will be good for all of us. She responded.

As she made her way to the front door, she noticed Daniel greeting people as they entered. She didn't think she could handle another interaction with him, so she timed her entry perfectly so that he was busy talking with a family on their way out of service. As she slipped by, she breathed a sigh of relief and made a beeline to the seat she had been sitting in for years.

"Hi, Cindy!" Angela was approaching from the front.

"Hello," Cindy stood and allowed Angela to give her a hug. She wanted to feel cared for, but she felt nothing. Still, it was nice.

"I'm glad you made it! Let's chat after service, okay?" Angela hustled off to take care of pastor's-wife things and Cindy sat back down.

The service went as usual. Worship, announcements, and the sermon. The pastor was talking about hope in the storm in today's message. Cindy wasn't sure she had that, but she was still trying, so that had to count for something.

As soon as the pastor bowed to close in prayer, Cindy gathered her things and headed for the door.

"I'm so glad I caught you!" Of course, Daniel was already at the door.

"Hello," she said as the inevitable bear hug wrapped around her. She brought one arm up and loosely hugged him back. It was surprising, and she pulled away.

He didn't seem to notice.

"How have you been?" he asked. His eyes held her attention. She felt the peace of God and something she couldn't identify when she was with him. Maybe it was joy, but she couldn't be sure.

"I have been good. Work has kept me busy." She lied.

"That's good."

"Hey, you two, we have to quit meeting this way!" Angela entered the lobby and greeted them both.

"Hi," was all Cindy could say. Standing here with two people whom she could almost see herself trusting was more than she could take, especially since one of them was a man.

"I actually need to get going," she lied again. "It was good to see you both." That was true, mostly.

"Good to see you too!" Angela said with a quick hug.

"Have a good week," Daniel replied with his usual smile.

Cindy avoided his eyes and hurried out the door.

"Back in the car," she mumbled to herself as she let out a breath, she didn't realize she was holding.

Her car was her safe place, and her home, of course. So many times, she had escaped from danger by running to one of these two places. They were all she had. She waffled between feeling grateful and feeling unprepared for life.

No place can ever truly feel safe.

We have this car and our home; those places are good.

Good, maybe, but we still cannot let our guard down.

Cindy didn't know how to respond to her inner concerns. There was danger everywhere. You could see it online, on TV, in her own town. How could she ever be anything more than someone who was always on the run from danger?

She started her car and shifted into reverse. Soon she was in the line of cars exiting the parking lot, but before she could get to the main road, her phone rang. "Hello?" she answered with one hand on the steering wheel and her phone in the other.

"Cindy?" It was Mrs. Watson.

"Um, yes?"

"I'm so sorry to call you on a Sunday."

"That's ok," Cindy had her blinker on and was waiting to turn.

"Brianna called in sick tomorrow, and I don't have anyone to cover. Do you think you could come to cover the early shift?"

Cindy had never done an early shift at the store before. Mornings were not really her thing.

"I can make that work." Why did she say that?

"Great, thank you so much! See you in the morning!"

With that, the call was over, and Cindy turned her car towards her house.

We can't do mornings!

I don't want to work.

We can't lose this job! We need it.

We always lose everything.

Cindy swatted away the voices and focused on the road. The rain had stopped, but the gray clouds remained. They were hanging low over the city for the entire drive home.

The little house on Swiss Street was waiting for her as expected. She had bought it when she was just out of college with money that her grandmother had left her when she died. She wasn't close to her mom's mom. In fact, she had only seen her a handful of times, but for some reason, she always had a soft spot for Cindy.

Thank God we have this place, she thought as she tossed her purse and keys on the table inside the door.

Her stomach growled, but she ignored it. She wandered aimlessly from room to room for a bit, and then she decided to head out back. Her yard was small and lined by a 4-foot wooden fence. Small bushes and shrubs were here and there. Hints at a tiny garden were at the edge of the patio. She had tried to grow peppers last year, but she just couldn't keep up with it.

She sat in a lawn chair that was on the small patio. The birdhouse was in plain view. As she looked at it, her mind drifted from this to that. The words from her Heavenly Father "I will be with you to the ends of the earth" drifted through her mind. They echoed in the back as she thought of everything she was going through.

"I don't know how to get out of this," she prayed out loud. "I know you are with me, and that seems like a greater gift than I could ever imagine, but somehow, it doesn't connect or relate to my life."

She paused as a robin landed on the edge of the little birdhouse exploring the home as an option for the spring. It soon flew off and landed in a nearby tree.

"I don't know," Cindy continued. "I guess I am able to access peace better than I used to. When I think about you being with me, it does calm me, but it doesn't seem to fix anything." She thought about all of the aspects of her life that brought her down, and her head dropped into her hands.

As if on cue, her parts joined in her conversation with God from a place deep in her soul.

Working is too hard for us! We are too little to work.

Nothing is safe! Can it ever be safe?

How will I ever do something useful when this is who I am?

Cindy's head tilted at that last thought. That was the truth of what she felt. She could get through every day. In fact, if she really, really let herself think about it, she was functioning way better than she had in her entire life. Her home was safe and comfortable. She had a few people she could call if she needed something - not that she would ever actually call them. But what she really wanted was to live for God. She wanted to be everything He made her to be and to bring him glory and honor. That didn't seem possible for a girl with her kind of story.

The sun was setting now, she wasn't exactly sure how long she had been out here.

Do you want to know now?

A question flashed through her mind.

Know what? She responded.

Why you never remember the evenings.

The voice was young and gentle. It was a little part of her mind trying to connect, trying to help her make sense of her crazy life.

I think so, Cindy replied with caution.

The part was hesitant, Cindy could feel it. *It's ok, you can tell me,* she encouraged.

It's because you are alone and feel like a failure every day. You don't see your purpose, so you just hide.

The words brought tears that Cindy couldn't cry. Her shoulders slumped, and she felt weak. The part was right, and they both knew it. There was nothing

Cindy could do.

She stood to head to her bed for the night. As she entered the house, a small bluebird landed on the brightly colored birdhouse in her yard, but she didn't see it.

Chapter 9

Monday morning came earlier than anyone expected.

"The early shift," Cindy muttered. "Why did I agree to this?"

At least the store doesn't open any earlier than 10:00 a.m., someone quipped.

"True," Cindy answered out loud.

As Cindy got ready for work, thoughts of the people in her life cycled through her mind. Mary, Angela, Mrs. Watson, and now Daniel. How did a man get on that list? It's not that she would say any of these people were actually safe – could anyone really be safe? But these four were different somehow. Only Mary knew the details of her trauma. Cindy didn't know what Mrs. Watson knew. Angela and Daniel didn't know anything about her past, but each person filled a need in her life.

Could it be that there are safe people out there? It's not possible!

But what if it is?

Cindy could barely handle the thoughts exploding in her mind, which made the drive to work almost intolerable. Walking through the doors of work was quite a relief. Her internal system knew the job was important and that Cindy would need to focus in order to keep it. The debate quieted down, and Cindy headed to the back to put her purse away.

"Good morning, Cindy!"

"Good morning, Mrs. Watson."

"Did you have a good weekend?"

"I did, thank you." Cindy shut the locker with her purse inside. She didn't want any other questions about the weekend, so she changed the subject. "How are things looking for the day?"

"Pretty good! Thank you again for covering for Brianna, I know this isn't your usual shift."

"No problem, I don't mind." Cindy and Mrs. Watson walked toward the sales floor, "what would you like me to do?"

"Well, Brianna usually starts the day by straightening inventory from the day before and making sure all of the registers have the supplies they need."

"No problem!"

Cindy checked the registers first and then began

organizing the racks of clothes and tables covered with purses and shelves of shoes and boots. She enjoyed the work. It was a nice change of pace from running the register.

The store opened, and customers came and went. Strange thoughts roamed through Cindy's mind all day. She would see a couple together and wonder if they were happy. She would see a mom and wonder if she was nice to her kids. She would see men and women shopping and wonder if they were good and kind or not. She had never really considered there might be different options for people. Cindy began to realize that she only ever had one category for people: unsafe.

This had left her alone and isolated for most of her life. Mary, Angela, Mrs. Watson, and even Daniel were contrary to her usual way of thinking.

What if not all people are bad?

Nausea crept into her stomach. The clock showed 2:00 p.m. She only had another hour left on her shift and then she could go home.

The next hour was a blur. Customers, credit cards, shoes, and dresses were all her world consisted of. She didn't remember much about that last hour or even if she did everything she was supposed to do.

Three o'clock finally rolled around, and Cindy

was glad. She retrieved her purse from her locker and headed to her car. As she started to drive, her thoughts started to open up again. She just listened.

People are too scary!

Not everyone, I like Mary, a little voice said.

Mary is okay for now, but maybe not for always.

Everyone makes mistakes, so no one can be safe.

We make the worst mistakes!

I know, we are not any more safe than anyone else.

The last statement surprised Cindy. She didn't feel like a safe person, but she had never really put that feeling into words before.

Does no one disagree with that? She asked.

We do.

Cindy could see a small group of children in her mind as she pulled up to her house. She waited in the car for them to finish.

We know Jesus is safe. He has taught us what it means to be kind.

That's true, someone else said.

Jesus is kind.

And fun!

If Jesus is kind, and we are all God's children, then others must be kind too.

Cindy had never thought of it that way before. She got out of the car and headed inside.

This changes everything.

Yes, it does.

That doesn't seem safe, change has never been good before.

Cindy cut off the conversation. One debate was enough for today, she didn't want to discuss the topic of change on top of safety!

The evening went well. When it was time for bed, Cindy decided to journal a bit more before falling asleep. "

Dear God, I don't know what is happening right now. Some days feel so much better than they used to, but some days are so much worse. I want to hold on to you in the good and in the bad, but I can't always remember."

She stopped to think for a moment.

Hezek reported a growing storm outside of the house.

Zral and Abel were singing praises to the Most High God.

"Thank you for the people you have put in my life, but mostly, thank you for being with me even when I can't do anything on my own. I trust you."

Cindy looked at the page. The last words she wrote were looking right back at her.

"I trust you."

I do trust Him.

We can't really trust anyone.

Who would help us? We are worthless.

Stupid! Trust is stupid!
No one can change who we are.
Trauma made me.

Cindy felt the lump growing in her throat. The lump that had been with her for her entire life. She knew there was a lot stored behind that lump, but she rarely saw it.

"I trust you, God." She said the words out loud to battle the voices rising in her mind.

Swords began to glow around the room. The spirit of God settled into the space allowing Cindy's mind to rest and her body to sleep.

She lay restfully in her bed for the first time in over a week. The sun was beginning to rise, and rays were shining from between a crack in her curtains onto the floor. A gentle breeze rustled the trees outside her home.

"She will sleep for a while," Michael said to Rabok and Salih who were sitting at her side.

Michael began to give instructions to the rest of his troops when suddenly he sensed a shift happening. He paused as did the rest of the angelic guard.

Everything was still. They didn't hear the birds outside. The clock was still working, but somehow the ticking was silent. Even the trees outside the little bedroom window were still.

Then, a loud crack pierced the silence. It was heard by every angelic being in the room and was followed by a boom that echoed through their ears and their spirits. Cindy didn't stir. Michael knew this sound came from the spiritual world. He shot up through the roof to see what was happening. Hezek and Kaleb came through the roof just behind him. They followed Michael's gaze to the north.

There, high in the sky, there was a giant dimple in the clouds. It was as if someone had dropped a huge rock into the pond and the water was dipping and receding in slow motion from its entry. Enormous ripples rolled from the center of the cloud outward. Michael and the others could feel the earth shake as each new ripple occurred.

"What is happening?" Hezek asked with his hand on his sword.

"A mighty warrior has taken their place in heaven," Michael said with deep respect in his voice.

"Fallen?" another warrior asked.

"Yes," Michael watched a ripple as it slowly washed through the clouds reaching the far ends of the city, "fallen to death."

"Did they fall at the hands of the enemy?" Hezek asked, still posed for battle.

"I don't know, but I do know that no warrior dies

in vain. God will use their death to strengthen all who turn to him in their time of grief." Michael pointed to the ripples, "you see, each ripple from the moment the earth lost his presence represents a move of the Lord, something being activated directly from the throne of God."

The angelic guard watched together. As each new ripple emanated from the core, the earth shook. As the ripple extended through the sky, the shake lessened to a vibration. Then the next ripple, the earth shook, and vibrations faded into the earth.

"I have never seen anything like this," an angel stated.

"Every fallen warrior has an impact on humanity for the sake of the Kingdom of God, but this is one the Lord must want us to be aware of." Then Michael noticed what was likely happening all along. Massive troops of angels were being dispatched all over the city with each ripple. He remembered with the first ripple seeing a downpour from the core directly down to the earth. Now he could see it clearly. Yes, each ripple carried warriors and ministering angels led by the power of the Holy Spirit into different areas of town.

One band was dropped at the church where Cindy attended. One was carried into a local business of some kind. Two bands were dropped into a neighborhood on the other side of town. A few of the ripples extended far onto the horizon, out of Michael's ability to see where they would end.

"God has used the death of this mighty warrior to fulfill a work that He and the warrior had begun," he paused in awe of the sight, "just like when Elijah took his place in heaven, and God granted Elisha a double portion of Elijah's anointing. A double portion of this warrior's anointing is being poured out on each of the people and places God has designated."

"But this is so much more than double," Hezek commented, watching darkness flee from all over the city at the arrival of warring angels.

"Maybe," Michael noted, "but we can be assured, whomever this warrior is, God is distributing their prayers and faith to bring the people of this community greater healing and connection to God."

Chapter 10

Cindy sat in session, unsure where to begin. "I just don't understand it," she said, as tears were streaming down her face. "He was so kind," she continued as she blew her nose, "for the first time in my life, I felt like I might be able to trust a man. Or at least talk to one." Cindy glanced up at Mary to gauge her reaction.

Mary was listening with such kindness in her eyes. Cindy continued.

"How could he have died like that? So suddenly?"

Mary waited for a moment before responding. As she waited the Holy Spirit settled into the room with knowledge and understanding.

"Cindy, I have a sense the Lord is doing something big, something new here."

"What could it possibly be?" Cindy wondered. "Daniel was so good for our church. I think he was good for me too."

Mary waited while Cindy transferred her

thoughts into words.

"I have been crying since I found out, but I'm not sure why. I barely knew him."

"He represented something to you, something important."

"I guess he did," Cindy was still reeling from the news.

Angela had called her yesterday afternoon to let her know that Daniel had died quite unexpectedly. She may have given Cindy more details than that, but Cindy couldn't remember. The only thing she remembered from the call was numbness. She completely numbed out to the words Angela was saying. She didn't even remember ending the call.

"I don't know why God would allow him to die like that." Cindy's head was in her hands. There was a growing pile of used Kleenex on her lap.

"I'm not sure either. Let's ask Him."

Cindy nodded, certain the Lord could never justify the loss of this great man to his family and to the community, but eager to see how God would respond.

She closed her eyes to turn her heart to the Lord. As she did, Ronan, Michael, and the others noticed their swords glowing. They instinctively put their hands to the handles. No demons appeared. There were no storm clouds forming, or evil of any kind nearby.

"The swords are simply reacting to the heavy presence of the Lord," Ronan informed the others. With that, each of them relaxed. They knew the Lord was present in an unusual way, and there would be no threats of danger.

"What is the Lord showing you, Cindy?" Mary asked patiently.

Cindy was quiet for a moment, and then, with her eyes still closed, she began to speak. "I see a figure. It's a man. I think it's Pastor Daniel," she winced, "he just collapsed on the floor." Cindy's forehead wrinkled, "I see Satan, he noticed and appears to be waiting to see what will happen," Cindy paused for a moment, and then continued, "as soon as Daniel collapsed, a smirk began to come over Satan's face. It was evil and dark." Cindy's face relaxed and her head tilted with interest, "but before the smirk could totally materialize, something happened. Something is happening." Cindy sat up a little straighter and leaned forward slightly as if trying to get a better look at a picture in her mind.

"Satan now looks completely terrified. He is frozen, and I think he is even shaking with fear," she paused, "wait, it looks like the earth is shaking." Cindy raised her eyebrows, and with her eyes still closed, she continued to report what she was seeing, "it is God. He is sending huge groups of angels forth with each tremble of the earth. Satan looks so scared. His eyes are darting back and forth at all that God is unleashing from the death of this man, from the death of Pastor Daniel.'"

The angels all over the room were now bowed before the presence of the Lord. The power of God was so great, no being could stand. The ministering angels wept as they saw what was unfolding all over the city. The worshiping angels hummed in low reverence as their faces were on the ground honoring the Sovereignty of the Most High God.

Cindy broke. Her shoulders began to heave as tears flowed freely down her face. She opened her eyes and looked at Mary. "It is both the most painful and the most beautiful thing I have ever seen." She took a deep breath, "I feel like Daniel's death released something powerful into this city. I saw a massive group of angels immediately descend on his family. The comfort and provision being released from heaven were enormous," she paused to remember more, "then I felt like the Lord said that prayers that Daniel uttered in his prayer room when no one could see or hear were being answered in supernatural ways."

"With each band of angels being released into the community, I could see cords of unity and strength being created and anointed by the Holy Spirit. It is as if God is bringing the body of Christ together for something new, something bigger than can be communicated in words."

Cindy sat quietly for a moment, stunned by all she had just seen. "Is this real?" she asked Mary.

"I know the presence of the Lord in this room right now is very real," Mary stated as a matter of fact. "I believe the Lord is showing you something very important, and you should hold it in your heart. God will help you understand more as you wait on Him."

"I know he will." Cindy wiped her eyes with a Kleenex and blew her nose. "I just can't believe Daniel is gone."

Mary and Cindy processed her emotions a little more before the session came to an end.

After the session, Cindy stopped by the grocery store on the way home. Her thoughts were torn between the sadness and grief of losing one of her pastors and the hope of God revealing the truth to her about what he was doing. Her typical response to these intense conflicts was to numb out. It was too difficult to feel, but she could numb out. Unfortunately, the numbing wasn't working as well as it used to.

As she tried to shut down all internal

conversations and the battle of her emotions, she just felt the weight of all of it. The despair and hope were indistinguishable. All emotions and thoughts morphed into a ball that was heavy and awkward to bear.

Who cares.

It's all too much.

Who cares about me, who cares about anything?

As Cindy walked through the store, the weight on her shoulders seemed to be increasing. Her feet were heavy and her thoughts, no longer racing, seemed to be stuck in sludge.

Each of the angels around her had swords drawn ready for the Lord to reveal the battle.

"Stay alert," Michael commanded.

Cindy put a box of cereal in the cart.

Things will never change.

There is nothing worse than this.

Cindy blocked out the sad commentary in her mind. She tossed a loaf of bread onto the small pile of groceries in the cart and headed to the register to check out. It seemed like there was something else she meant to get, but there was no energy to remember. As she approached the register, she felt her body get tense. Her ears were hearing something, but she had no awareness of what it was. She raised her head and her mind focused on the conversation happening in front of her.

"I don't really care what that ad says, the sign said this was on sale. I demand the sale price." The short woman was glaring at the cashier.

"I understand, I told you I would be happy to call a manager and…."

"I don't want you to call a manager. You should be able to handle this yourself!" one hand was on her hip and the other was waving an angry finger towards the cashier.

Cindy could feel her heartbeat increasing.

You have to get out of here!

This isn't safe!

No, be still, be quiet, and don't draw attention to yourself.

Cindy closed her eyes.

Red scarf.

She didn't know where that thought came from.

Red scarf.

It had a different feel than her own thoughts.

Daniel.

Her shoulders relaxed slightly.

A chill ran over her arms. She felt a strange strength for just an instant, and then it was gone. She looked at the cashier who was still being criticized by the short woman with a big attitude, but this time she really saw the cashier. The girl was young, maybe seventeen. She was sinking low.

Cindy could see the tears beginning to well in her eyes.

What would Daniel have done if that were me? The thought flew through her mind in an instant.

What would I want someone to do for me? The thoughts were flashing through faster than she could think them.

In a moment, without thinking, she caught the cashier's attention and gave her a warm, knowing smile. It was genuine and pure. She knew exactly what that young girl was feeling. It felt like she held her eyes for minutes, but she knew it was just a second. At that moment, Cindy felt her body relax a little more. In her mind's eye, she saw a quick flash in her DNA. The same picture from the vision God gave her months ago. A strand of black yarn that was entangled in her bloodline, loosened. It was barely holding on now.

The cashier's shoulders straightened slightly. She turned from the angry woman and picked up the speaker to call for a manager. In a few minutes, the manager was there and taking care of the matter. As Cindy reached the register, the young girl gave her a sheepish smile. "Thanks," she said as she scanned Cindy's items.

Cindy just nodded and smiled back. She really wasn't sure what to say, but she felt just a little lighter than when she came in.

"What just happened," Gabe asked Michael.

Michael was smiling from ear to ear. "She made a blow to the darkness."

"How? What did she do?" Gabe was clearly confused as were a few other angels.

"She is breaking through generational holds on her," Michael was still smiling as he put his sword back in the sheath, "she used the fruit of the Spirit, kindness, and broke through the darkness that was over-taking that young woman, and that broke the darkness that Cindy was drowning in herself. It was a holy moment."

Cindy was finishing her transaction, as the angels looked back at her with a sense of curiosity and awe.

"That's all it takes?" asked Gabe.

"That is certainly part of it," Michael started, "she has been breaking through her own darkness already. Just now, she chose to align with God by choosing to have a different response to this intense situation than what was normal for her. Instead of retreating into herself, she chose to see the cashier through God's eyes. In doing that, she took a stand against the generational inheritance of apathy that had plagued her family line, and the Holy Spirit flowed through her choice to break the darkness."

Gabe was beginning to understand. "That's

amazing how simple it can be."

"God's truth is simple but powerful."

On the drive home, Cindy felt the ball of indifference begin to unwind. She wasn't sure what the change was, but she knew there was one. The emotions she was feeling earlier became more defined once again, and she was able to hold them and even identify them.

"I care."

She heard the words in her heart and the tears instantly burst through the lump in her throat and rolled down her cheeks. She pulled over into a parking lot and let the tears flow.

"I care." The words were now a memory but still held power. She knew Jesus had spoken the words to her heart. If He cares, then she cares. She has his love and his power in her.

I don't feel it, I just want to feel him.

It isn't about feelings, it's about faith. It's about who you are.

Cindy tilted her head. That last thought was new. Never had she recognized that her feelings impacted her faith so much. But should they?

"Jesus, help me understand," she prayed as she wiped her face on the edge of her sleeves. The tears were subsiding as this new mystery and truth began to fill her mind.

She waited in silence for the Lord to speak again. With all her might, she turned her ears toward God for truth and understanding. She didn't know if God said those words about faith and feelings or if it came from her own heart, but it felt powerful and true. She just wanted to understand.

Silence.

After a few minutes, her shoulders dropped. The tension that was building from her intense listening was released. Disappointment.

"Why won't you answer?"

"I'm sorry," she didn't want to doubt or question God. She just didn't understand God's ways. With thoughts of confusion and doubt, she drove home and started making dinner.

Chapter 11

"I just don't know what he is thinking these days," Darlene was sitting on the back patio of her farmhouse with her phone pressed to her ear. "He barely speaks, and when he does, well, let's just say he isn't very nice."

The patio had enough seating for a dozen people when it wasn't set up for a party. The outdoor fireplace was lit this morning to fight off the cool air outside. Not one leaf, branch, or smudge of dirt was on the stone floor that made up the 500-square-foot outdoor living space. A large TV was hung on the wall closest to the house where Derek would often watch sporting events or news. It was unusually quiet in the backyard today. Spring was a time for birds and wildlife to come alive, especially in the country, but not today.

"Oh, he is coming, got to go!" She hung up the phone quickly as Derek joined her on the patio.

"Good morning," she said.

"Who was that?" he responded.

"Just my sister," Darlene said, trying to sound casual. "She is having a hard time with her kids right now, you know, the usual." She tried to smile, but it just didn't feel right.

"That's her own fault," he said coldly as he sat down and started scrolling on his phone.

"Would you like some breakfast, sir?" the young cook asked as she approached the table.

"My usual," he stated without looking up.

"Yes, sir," she replied and hurried off to the kitchen.

Darlene didn't even know how to talk to her husband these days. Things had always been tense between them, but the past few weeks had been unbearable. She didn't know what was happening.

"So, I visited the school in town a few days ago," she said to no response. "You know, the one that was flooded a few weeks back?"

"Uh-huh," he replied, staring at his phone as she spoke.

"They are looking for a few more donations so they can finish the repairs." She paused, still nothing. "The children have been meeting in that big catholic church for classes since the school shut down, and it really isn't suitable for."

"They are irresponsible with money," Derek

interrupted. "They could have had that entire building fixed by now if they knew what they were doing." His tone was cold but steady. He still didn't look up from his phone.

"That may be true, but it would be nice to help the children at least," she replied, knowing she was crossing the line. He had already given a verdict on the situation, and he was not one to change his mind.

Derek stood up, without taking his eyes off his phone, and replied, "I don't want you helping them. I don't want breakfast anymore either. I lost my appetite."

He left the room. Chills went down Darlene's spine. Derek had a way of stabbing her heart over and over again without ever raising his voice or saying a harsh word. She knew what he meant. After decades of living with his tactics, there was no doubt what each word meant, and it was rarely good.

The cook came back with Derek's breakfast and started to put it on the table.

"Stupid girl," Darlene spewed. "Can you not see he left! He won't be eating breakfast this morning."

The girl froze for a moment, unsure what to do.

"Well, clean this mess up already!" Darlene yelled as she stood up and stormed into the house. "You just can't find good help these days!"

Within seconds Darlene was in the foyer of the large home. She grabbed her car keys and purse and stormed out, slamming the door behind her.

Anger and rage dripped from her and melted into the growing piles of tar and gunk all over the property. It was nothing new. Nothing about her situation was new, and she hated it! She hated him, and everything he represented. She would help the school, whether he liked it or not.

As she left the property, her mind started to clear a bit. She needed to be able to think, and she couldn't do that there with him. She decided to visit her beautiful Azalea Pathway on the way into town. It was peaceful there, and maybe it would help. She didn't want to bust into the church angry at her husband. In fact, she was determined to be the sweetest, kindest person they ever met.

I will show him who makes the decisions around here! She thought to herself.

It was strange to her how easily she could feel the hate and anger in her heart. She used to be able to manage it so much better. She could even hide it from herself. These days, it was tossed around carelessly on anyone nearby. Thoughts that she usually kept to herself, judgments that were for her and her small group of friends, were now spoken with bitterness and anger to anyone who would listen.

I must get this under control.

Before she knew it, she had arrived at the church. *Wait, I don't remember seeing the Azaleas,* she thought. A flash of Azalea Pathway went through her mind. *Oh yes, I did.*

Her incessant determination to be better than her husband and to prove something to herself had overtaken her thoughts, and she had missed the entire road of her favorite trees.

"He truly does ruin everything," she muttered.

Just before she entered the church building, she stopped and took a deep breath to calm herself. "Pull it together, Darlene," she chided herself.

She pulled the door open and was immediately greeted by an older woman sitting at the front desk.

"Good morning! How can we help you today?" she said with a smile.

"Good morning," Darlene adjusted her blouse, "my name is Darlene, and I met with Pastor Jacobs last week, about the school? Anyways, I was wondering if he is in today." She could hear the sharpness in her tone, but she was helpless to change it.

"He is!" the woman smiled and picked up the phone as she spoke. "Give me a minute and I will let him know you are here."

Darlene took a seat near the door in what looked like an office chair straight from the 80s. It was comfortable enough. As she waited, she continued to try to calm her thoughts, but before she could make much progress, the office door in the back opened.

"Good morning!" Mrs. Jacobs came out of the back office and approached Darlene with her hand out.

"Good morning," Darlene shook her hand. "I came to speak to Pastor Jacobs about the school situation."

"Wonderful!" she smiled warmly. "He is in a meeting right now, but I'd be happy to talk with you." She motioned toward a small room off the main lobby and the two walked in that direction. "It is good to see you again."

"Likewise," Darlene was usually very good at small talk, but the raging battle inside made it difficult to focus.

"How about all of this rain we have been having, kind of crazy, isn't it!" Mrs. Jacobs was clearly trying to engage with Darlene, unsuccessfully.

"I suppose."

They entered the small office, and Darlene claimed a chair just inside the door. Mrs. Jacobs sat down across from her. A small band of angels assigned to Mrs. Jacobs followed them in with swords drawn and ready for battle. The evil binding Darlene was clear to each of them, and it was their job to protect the pastor's wife, as well as open any doors to the Holy Spirit to reach the heart of this lost woman.

"So, what can I do for you?" Mrs. Jacobs asked pleasantly.

"Well, I have been thinking about the school, and the situation those poor kids are in," Darlene started. "And I really want to help,"

"Excellent!"

"My husband is unsure about the situation though, and so I am trying to get a better understanding of exactly what is needed." She didn't want to bring Derek into the conversation, why did she say that?

"I see," Mrs. Jacobs was kind and patient in her response, "it is important for husbands and wives to be on the same page with these sorts of things." She leaned back casually in her chair, almost inviting Darlene to tell her more.

"I mean, it's not like we disagree, we just have a different way of looking at things," Darlene stated, but she didn't really know where she was going with this. "He is very pragmatic, and I, well, I just like to do the right thing, you know." She could feel her blood pressure rising, and the raging storm inside started to push its way to the surface.

"Is it warm in here?" she asked the pastor's wife.

"I can turn a fan on if you'd like?"

"No, no, it's fine. Where was I? Oh, yes, my marriage is fine." She gave a weak smile. She had no idea what she was talking about or where this conversation was going, but she knew she was about to burst.

"It sounds like you have a lot going on right now," Mrs. Jacob empathized. "We can talk about whatever you would like. It doesn't have to be about the school."

There it was. The actual invitation to open up. Darlene was determined not to share her personal business with anyone outside of the home, but she wasn't sure she could stop it. Something about Mrs. Jacobs and her kindness drew it out of her, and without thinking she burst into tears. Years of anger, resentment, and hate poured from her while the kind pastor's wife sat and listened, offering an occasional "I'm so sorry" or "that must have been really hard."

All around the room a battle ensued. The darkness that filled the room as Darlene spoke was thick and smelled like burning tar, and it had fought long and hard to keep the anger and hate buried in Darlene's heart. It would do anything to keep the light of God from reaching her. Mrs. Jacobs angelic guard was holding their ground though, allowing Mrs. Jacobs to be used by the Lord to minister to this lost woman.

"Stand your ground," the lead angel instructed.

Swords flew and demons were crushed right and left. Still, the evil kept pouring out from this woman who was baring her soul. At some point, Mrs. Jacobs said a silent prayer for wisdom and protection. When that happened, the swords around the small room began to glow, and the power of God fell on the prayer room.

"Watch her," the lead angel told the ministering angels. "There is about to be an opening."

Every spiritual being in the room could see the tight, tar-coated leather jacket that bound and restricted Darlene from finding freedom. They knew the Lord was doing something powerful, and they were ready to cooperate with his plan.

"I just don't know what to do sometimes," Darlene had paused again to blow her nose and dry her face. The box of Kleenex by her chair was almost empty.

"I can understand that," Mrs. Jacobs replied, this was the first Mrs. Jacobs had spoken in quite a while. "I know there is a lot happening for you right now, and I know one prayer won't fix it all, but do you mind if I say a prayer for you?"

Darlene eyed her suspiciously. Evil voices whispered threats and despair into her ears, and she wondered what angle this woman was playing. But she was at the end of her rope and couldn't continue this way anymore.

What could it hurt?

The thought blew through her mind like a whisper, but somehow it was still loud enough to silence all the other thoughts.

With hesitation she responded. "I suppose."

At that, Mrs. Jacobs bowed her head, closed her eyes, and led by the Holy Spirit, she began to pray.

The instant her mouth opened, the ministering angels saw a crack appear in the leather binding.

"Now!" The lead angel directed.

In a flash, two ministering angels stabbed their glowing swords into the crack which had begun oozing putrid black smoke and tar. Three warring angels who had joined the room mid-battle took positions around Darlene to subdue any evil that would try to escape.

"I ask that you comfort this woman's heart," Mrs. Jacobs continued, "and bring her to a place of knowing you and your grace."

The crack widened as Mrs. Jacobs continued.

The swords of the ministering angels were now consumed with fire from heaven that instantly absorbed the putrid evil that was leaking from the leather jacket. Around the room, the song of the worshiping angels could now be heard above the clanging of swords and daggers. Either the battle was decreasing, or the power of the Lord was growing. No one knew which, but it didn't matter. The Most High God was winning this battle.

"In Jesus' name we pray, Amen." Mrs. Jacobs opened her eyes and grabbed a Kleenex to wipe her own tears. She glanced up at Darlene. Dried tear stains were on her face, and she looked a little shell-shocked, but definitely more peaceful than when she walked in. "Are you okay?"

"I am, I think." It took a moment for Darlene to regain her composure. She had never experienced anything like that before. "I really should be going." It was all a bit much for her. She gathered her things and stood to leave.

"I understand," Mrs. Jacobs started. She reached out and touched Darlene's arm. "I just want you to know we are here for you. If you ever need anything, I'll be glad to come and do what I can."

"Thank you, I will be fine." Darlene forgot about the school. She forgot about Derek and about the many fights over the decades. She forgot about everything that was important to her as she hurried out the door.

"Follow her out until the Lord is done," the warrior angel told the ministering angels. "Her permission for Mrs. Jacobs to pray is all we needed to fight for her salvation. It is now the Holy Spirit who will draw her. Ultimately, it will be her choice to receive that salvation or not."

As she sat in her car in the parking lot of the small church, Darlene wept. She wept like she had never wept before. All the years of pain, neglect, and abuse were building up inside and exploding out of the crack in her leather jacket like a volcano on the verge of eruption. One ministering angel continued to keep his sword stabbed into the leather bondage, absorbing the evil it released, while the other kept watch around the car to ensure there were no unwelcome visitors to this holy moment.

Darlene knew who God was. She had been to church most of her life. Of course, she would never attend a small church like this one, it was too hard to blend in here, but she knew of God.

Tears continued to stream down her face as her mind went through the different memories of pain and sorrow that she had experienced throughout her life. There were so many times she wished she had made a different choice, gone a different direction, or married a different man. The wailing started again as she allowed the truth about her husband into her heart. She could not bear to think of it. In fact, she had chosen not to think of it for most of her marriage.

I must get out of here, she thought as her anxiety and panic began to rise. She knew Derek would be furious if he knew she went back to the church after he told her not to.

She didn't take the long way home. The thought of Azalea Pathway was nowhere in her mind. As her tears clouded her vision, she drove as quickly as she could out of town and into the countryside. Within a few minutes, her car was sitting at the end of the farmhouse driveway. A few more chest heaves and two Kleenex later, she knew she had to make a choice.

The glowing sword of the ministering angel was still piercing the leather jacket binding Darlene. The two warring angels that followed her home were aware they were on the edge of the evil filled property. Darkness glared at them from across the property line, but the power of God held it at bay.

Darlene took one long, deep breath. She must compose herself if she was going to go back into that home.

Do I have to go home? Do I really have to?

Thoughts went through her mind of leaving her husband. Leaving the darkness she felt around her every day, leaving the world of agony and pain she had known for the past four decades.

Where would I even go?

Thoughts of her mother's cottage down south rolled through her mind. She hadn't been to that old cottage in years. It was always available to her though – as well as to the rest of the family. She could go there. She could start new, and maybe find a better life for herself. Maybe she would even be able to contact her daughter. She missed Cindy dearly, but there had been no communication between them for many months.

A strange peace started to settle over her heart.

The crack in her leather jacket began to widen ever so slightly.

Her mind was still for an instant, a very rare, but precious instant.

As she looked up at the house, one word came to mind: Derek.

Evil spat at the angels standing guard around the car.

Derek.

The crack in the leather was becoming unstable.

What would Derek say? What would he do? He had

given her the life she always wanted. Okay, maybe not the life she always wanted, but all the things she always wanted.

She ran her hand around the steering wheel of her blue Cadillac. Even this car. He had given it to her as an anniversary gift several years ago. She was severely depressed that year, and was debating moving out of the house. Come to think of it, she had wanted to go to her mom's cottage back then too. Then Derek had this beautiful car delivered, and she was smitten once again. She couldn't leave him.

She knew all too well what this choice to stay would mean for her. While Derek had his moments of kindness, they were few and far between.

The crack in the leather began to quake ever so slightly.

As Darlene thought of all the abuse and torment she had received from her husband over the years, her heart began to fill with hate.

One of the evil entities broke ranks and darted towards the car. He was gone in an instant as a glowing sword slashed through him.

The cottage. The one last peaceful thought that Darlene had before she allowed the thoughts of hate and bitterness to overtake her.

I will not let him get away with all he has done to me!

Leave him with this beautiful house and all the things we have built over the years? I don't think so! He doesn't deserve them!

She shifted her car into drive.

"We are losing her!" the ministering angels shouted to the warring angels who were now in battle around the car.

"Keep holding on!" one responded. "As long as she doesn't cross into the driveway, we will fight!"

The demons were flying at the car now, one by one trying to gain entrance. The warriors held them off giving the Holy Spirit the space needed to draw her to God.

Derek.

Darlene's face twisted, and she moved her foot from the brake to the gas pedal.

As she crossed the property line into the driveway, the sword that was reaching her heart popped out of the leather. The crack was closed in an instant, and Darlene was gone, driving back into the darkness where she had lived for far too long.

The three angelic beings lingered at the edge of the property. The darkness didn't care about them anymore. They had their prize.

"What will happen to her now," the ministering angel asked.

"We cannot know," the warring angel said with

sadness. "She has made her choice."

At that, the three of them returned to the small church to report what happened, and to continue with their assigned care of the body of Christ.

Chapter 12

Saturday morning greeted Cindy with a headache. The day before she had barely made it through work. She didn't want to go, but there was too much on her mind to stay at home. She had hoped the work would keep her mind off Daniel, her shame, and her life. It didn't.

As she rolled over and looked at the clock, she realized she needed to leave for work in just a few moments.

She couldn't. Not today.

She picked up her phone and sent Mrs. Watson a quick email. She had told her yesterday that a friend died, and Mrs. Watson had encouraged her to take some time off if needed. Today it was needed.

She laid in bed for a few moments rehearsing the last few days.

Definitely a roller coaster, she thought.

Mary had told her on Thursday that they could meet again on Saturday if needed. At the time, it didn't seem necessary, but now it felt like the only safe option for the day.

There is that word again.

I know.

She sent Mary a text asking if the late morning slot was still available. It was, so Cindy told her she would be in soon.

What's the big deal?

You didn't even know him.

You don't deserve to have this kind of pain over a man you didn't even know. Think of his family! They have it really bad.

It was confusing. Why did it matter so much? She really didn't know him. The red scarf man. Strange how such few interactions could make such a big difference.

A moan escaped her lips as she sat up and put her feet on the floor. With her head in her hands, she prayed: God, please help me get through this, whatever this is.

With another small burst of strength, she stood and wobbled to the kitchen to get some aspirin and coffee. She might even drink some water too. Anything to make this headache go away.

She carried her two drinks, pills, and a pastry she had bought at the store the day before back to her bedroom and sat on her bed.

One hour before we have to leave, she told herself.

Why is Mary doing this? Why does she even care?

Why does Mrs. Watson care? It isn't that big of a deal?

Or is it, Cindy wondered.

After a few minutes, the coffee was gone and so was the pastry. She used the water to take the aspirin but didn't drink more than needed.

Get dressed, she ordered herself.

Another moan escaped as she pushed herself up from the bed and walked to her closet. It felt like she was wearing a padded coat. The weight on her body was heavy and she found it difficult to lift her arms. Her brain was thick with fog, but she pushed through to find a pair of sweats and a t-shirt to wear to counseling. It didn't really matter what she wore. Mary had seen her at her worst, and she was certain she wouldn't be going anywhere after counseling.

The drive to Mary's office was uneventful. Cindy didn't remember most of it. As she went into the waiting room to sit down, she had the strangest feeling. It was difficult to put a word to it.

Purpose.

The word didn't come from her.

Purpose.

There it was again.

It wasn't a word Cindy thought about often. Truthfully, it was too painful. The word had always been tied to either darkness or hopelessness.

I suppose those two words are the same, Cindy thought.

The waiting room was a simple space. The carpet was dark gray and a little worn. Big windows lined the outside wall, and a row of simple chairs lined the windows. Across from the chairs was a small loveseat. This was Cindy's seat of choice. From here she could see out the window. She could see people coming and going in the front door on her left, and she could see Mary's door down the small hallway to her right.

Darkness or hopelessness.

What a terrible choice! How could anyone choose between these two things for their purpose? She wondered.

The vision last fall had given her hope there could be something more. As faded pictures of the vision rolled through her mind, she remembered how she felt that day. For the first time in her life, she felt like an overcomer! She felt like God was revealing his purpose for her, something she could do for him, It was wonderful.

Wonderful. Another strange word she rarely used.

"Cindy, are you ready?" Mary's head poked out of her office.

Cindy nodded and followed Mary into the comfortable counseling room.

"I'm glad you sent me the text," Mary started

after the usual chit-chat and opening prayer.

Cindy was glad Mary started sessions so slowly. Especially since the session usually got heavy fast.

"Yeah, I appreciate you offering it." Cindy wasn't sure where to start.

"How have the last few days been?" Mary inquired.

"Interesting," Cindy thought for a moment. It was hard to remember. Then the incident at the grocery store came to mind. She told Mary the story.

"It was so strange," Cindy said after telling Mary about what had happened in the grocery store, "it was like I could see the woman demanding the red scarf. I could see Daniel, and then I could feel, well, I felt my heart. I'm not sure if I have ever felt my heart before."

"That sounds like it was a powerful moment. A lot was happening," Mary affirmed.

"Yes, there was a lot happening," Cindy seemed surprised at the thought. "I didn't see it that way at the time. In one moment, I was just trying to survive and in the next, I was seeing the cashier and hearing," she paused, "I think I was hearing God's voice. I think he was reminding me of what Daniel did."

The two sat in silence for a moment.

Around them the worshiping angels were

exalting God in song, as the ministering angels were surrounding both Mary and Cindy, creating space for the Holy Spirit to breathe life into the room.

"I have wanted to help people, I have wanted to do something big for God, but this felt big. I mean, it felt really big." Cindy was focused on a spot on the floor as she searched for her next words. "I didn't know such a small act could be so big." She pulled her legs up on the couch sitting crisscross applesauce and turned to make eye contact with Mary. "It reminds me of the parable of the Good Shepherd with his sheep. The ONE sheep that wandered off was important to the shepherd. That was his BIG act that day was saving the ONE. That is what it felt like in the store. I helped the ONE. That's what Daniel did for me, and I think that is what Jesus would have done too," Cindy concluded.

"I think you are right," Mary began, "In fact, I think that is what Jesus does every day. He looks for the ONE. You are the ONE, I am the ONE, he is searching for each ONE of us. He is fighting for each of us."

Cindy nodded in agreement.

"One more thing," she started, "I saw something when it happened. It was just a flash, but it was very vivid."

"What did you see?"

"Do you remember the vision the Lord gave me last fall?"

"Yes, the one with the DNA, right?" Mary asked.

"That's the one."

Mary nodded.

"Well, I saw my DNA, at least that is what I think it was, and something black loosened from it. I mean, I could tell it wasn't really attached to begin with, but it was entwined, tangled up with me. It became very loose." Cindy was quiet for a moment as if she was seeing it again in her mind's eye. "What do you think it means?"

"Let's ask Jesus," Mary responded.

Cindy nodded, and as the two closed their eyes, darkness began to overtake the room. Michael, Ronan, and their guards were surprised for a moment. They were each so enraptured in Cindy's story and in the power of the Most High God, they forgot they could be in battle at any moment.

Ronan was the first to have his sword drawn, but Michael was a close second. The worshiping angels kept singing as the rest of the troops armed themselves and took their positions close to Cindy and Mary and around the perimeter of the room.

The darkness didn't advance. It seemed as surprised to be revealed as the angelic guard was to be seeing it. The spiritual beings all stood frozen, quiet, waiting on the first move to be made.

Mary began to pray. "Father God, thank you for the work you are doing to heal and cleanse Cindy's bloodline. Thank you for allowing her to flow with your Spirit in helping the young woman at the grocery store," Mary paused with silent gratitude for the Lord.

The evil entities around the room were still, but ready to launch at a moment's notice.

"What is holding them?" Gabe asked with his sword out and his posture poised for battle.

Michael and Ronan answered together. "The power of God."

"We would like to ask what the vision means that Cindy saw when she helped that young woman. What would you like us to know about it, God?"

A few of the demons began to growl and utter aggressive sounds.

"I see the same image, the one from the grocery store," Cindy was quiet.

Mary was praying quietly.

Each of the angelic guards had their eye on their assigned enemy, ready for battle, but waiting for the command.

The enemy of the Most High God stood, paralyzed or choosing not to move, no one knew which.

As Mary prayed, the tension in the room increased, but no one moved. There was an unusual stillness in the space. Mary was familiar with it, but it was new to Cindy. She sat motionless with her eyes closed just waiting on the Lord.

"Purpose." This time the word was almost audible.

"Purpose." She could see the letters float through her mind. They felt light and airy while also seeming to be solid and reliable.

"I had this word go through my mind in the waiting room a few minutes ago, and it keeps going through my mind right now. I don't know what it means though," Cindy started.

"What is the word?"

"Purpose." Cindy opened her eyes and fidgeted with the hem of her shirt.

"Interesting," Mary started, "what does that word mean to you?"

"I don't really know." Cindy scanned the room. "I loved my corporate job, but it didn't feel like my purpose. In the end, I couldn't do it anyway." Her eyes settled on the tropical plant soaking up light by Mary's big picture window. "I have always wanted a purpose, you know, a calling, but I don't know what it could possibly be."

"So, purpose means 'calling' to you?" Mary

clarified.

"I guess," Cindy shrugged. "What else could it mean?"

Mary tilted her head as she thought for a moment. "Let's ask God about that."

Cindy was hesitant, although she didn't know why. "Okay," was all she said before she closed her eyes again.

The evil entities around the room continued to be at an eerie stillness. The angelic guard continued to stand ready.

"Father God, what do you want Cindy to know about the word purpose," Mary paused.

Cindy cringed as the first picture entered her mind.

"What do you see," Mary asked.

"My birth," Cindy started. "God has shown me this moment before," she waited a moment. "There is so much darkness around me, I can't make out any details or people, just the weight of the darkness."

They both sat in silence waiting for the Lord.

Cindy tilted her head with curiosity. "Something is different with the picture this time." After another moment, "there is a light, a very bright light shining from above me somewhere. It is captivating!" She was quiet for a few minutes.

"Kind of mesmerizing. It is warm and bright, and," she thought about it. "Holy, the light is very holy."

Mary made a few notes in her notepad. "What else?"

"Oh," Cindy said with surprise, "a tiny dot of that holy light is in me!" She was quite surprised by this revelation. "It is like a seed. A seed that the bright light planted in me at conception. It had been growing with me the whole time, it was just now big enough to see it." Cindy leaned forward a bit as she kept watching.

"I see myself growing up, fast-forwarding through my life. The seed is still there. It grows a little now and again, but it is close to the same size as it was when I first saw it. So much darkness is happening all around me, but I couldn't focus on it even if I tried. The seed has, well, it has me. It's like it is the only thing that matters."

"Wow," Mary commented, "what else?"

"The huge bright light above me is always there, at a distance, but always there. Well, now I am at the age where I received the Lord as my Savior. It was a powerful moment."

"I remember, we have talked about it before," Mary commented.

"At that moment, the seed in me reached for the Light," Cindy's eyebrows rose in awe. "The Light reached back! It touched me. In fact, it joined with the seed." Cindy was relaxed again on the couch, but completely captivated by the scene unfolding in her mind.

The darkness in Mary's office was starting to get irritated but still wasn't moving.

"We are connected now. The seed in me and the Light from above. And somehow the light seems a little brighter than it was before. Like it was happy to finally be with me." Cindy watched for a few more minutes, "I continue to grow, and the darkness continues to swirl around me, but the solid connection I have with the Light is kind of unbelievable. No matter what happens around me, what happens to me, it doesn't change. It doesn't weaken or lessen. In fact, at moments it seems like it might be getting stronger." Cindy opened her eyes abruptly. She sat in stunned silence.

Mary gave her a few minutes before speaking. "That sounds like it was quite powerful."

"It was," was all Cindy could say. When she had a few moments to process, she began to describe her experience to Mary. "I think the Lord was trying to tell me that he planted his spirit in me from the time I was conceived. It was always there."

"I believe that is true, Cindy," Mary affirmed.

"He followed me throughout my life wanting to

connect with me, waiting, I don't know, for me to want him." Cindy paused, wanting to remember all she had experienced. "Then I saw the moment I received him as Lord and Savior. At that moment, we connected! The light that was in me reached out to him like I was choosing him," Cindy gave a sheepish smile. "I guess that is what salvation is."

Mary smiled. "Yes, it is."

"Anyways, I chose him, and he was so happy about it. It was strange though," Cindy mused.

"What?"

"In that moment, in the moment my little seed of light connected with God the Father, I saw the word 'purpose' flash through my mind." Cindy paused, "I felt complete in that moment. I don't think I felt that when I got saved, but I felt it just now." She stopped to ponder what it might mean. "I think my purpose was to connect with God. My purpose is to connect with God," she looked at Mary. "Could it be that simple?"

Mary smiled and put her pen down, "why, yes, I think it is that simple. God created us in his image for a relationship with him. When we find him as Lord and Savior, the Bible says the angels rejoice! I believe this is because the Lord is rejoicing. It is a beautiful day in the Kingdom of God."

Cindy was smiling as well; she couldn't help it.

Around her, the angels were still standing ready for a fight as the darkness in the room had not yet been impacted by what God was revealing.

"Why haven't they left or even moved," Gabe questioned. He was posed for a fight; he had been for almost an hour now.

Ronan studied the room, "Whatever is keeping them here has not been broken yet, there is more the Lord is doing."

"Stay on alert, but I don't think there will be much battle for us to fight when the Lord is done," Michael added.

"I do have one question," Cindy added. "What does the purpose of salvation have to do with my day-to-day life? I mean, of course, salvation is the purpose God designed for each of us, but then what? You can't make a calling out of getting saved, and there is still plenty of life to live after salvation. So how does this purpose relate to my everyday life?"

"That's a good question!" Mary replied, "Let's pray about it."

They both bowed their heads to pray. The demons began to get ever more agitated as Light began to drift into the room.

"Father God, what would you like Cindy to know about her day-to-day purpose?" Mary inquired.

Cindy waited on the Lord. After a moment her head tilted, and her eyebrows went up. Then she smiled and gave a slight nod. When she opened her eyes, there was a special light on her face and a tone in her voice that was new and full of life.

"What did he tell you?" Mary asked with a big smile.

"At first I wasn't sure what He was saying," Cindy started. "I saw a calendar. Day by day started to go by and then month by month and then year by year. Then I saw that tiny seed of light that was in my heart appear on each day of the calendar. Just as the tiny seed appeared, I saw the holy light appear above the calendar," she paused to think about the picture.

Mary was taking notes on her notepad as Cindy continued.

"I could see the little seed of light on each day reaching for the light above. It was like it knew it needed the light. It wanted to be connected to the light," she blushed slightly, "I wanted to be connected to the light, to God's light. Every time the seed reached to connect the light of God met it. There was a sense of deep satisfaction in each day, each connection, each moment of being together. It was beautiful."

"That sounds beautiful, Cindy."

"I'm still not entirely clear on what this means about my purpose though," Cindy confessed.

Mary thought for a moment. "Could it be that the Lord designed you for connection? Specifically for connection with Him? Maybe your purpose each and every day is to connect with the Lord. He wants to be in a relationship with you."

"Could that be true?"

"Of course, it could! You are his daughter, and he loves you."

"But there is nothing special about me. In fact, there is a lot of terrible about me."

"It doesn't matter how you see yourself or what you have been through, you are still his daughter. Connecting with him brings life to each of us, and it brings us to Him. It is a beautiful thing!"

Cindy was starting to smile again, "so how do I choose him every day? I don't think that means I get saved every day, right?"

Mary laughed. "You are right. What do you think it looks like to choose him every day? To connect with him every day?"

Cindy considered the question. "Well, I think it is what I am doing now. I choose him when I am struggling. I am thankful when I am struggling and when I am not. I try to honor him with my choices."

"That absolutely sounds like choosing him. Why

do you think choosing him is so important?" Mary asked.

"I don't know actually," Cindy thought about Mary's question. "I know it is the only way I can survive. I wouldn't be here today if it weren't for him. I just hope surviving isn't my only purpose in life." Cindy was starting to feel a little discouraged, and the demons around the room were starting to move a bit.

"Oh, I don't think that's your only purpose," Mary replied. "What do you think God gets from you choosing him?"

"I don't know. I never really thought of it."

"Let's ask him," Mary closed her eyes and asked the Father why it was important to him that Cindy choose him every day.

After several minutes of silence, Cindy looked up. "Nothing."

"What were you experiencing while you were quiet?" Mary asked.

"Nothing. It was just quiet."

"What were you thinking about?"

"Nothing really," Cindy paused. "Except, you know that light I connected with as a seed?"

Mary nodded.

"Well, I think I just saw that light. It just got really, really bright."

"What do you think that means? Cindy inquired.

"I have no idea," Cindy stated. "It didn't seem important, so I almost didn't mention it, but I can still see it, even with my eyes open. It is SO BRIGHT now," Cindy emphasized.

Mary was smiling. "Cindy, have you ever thought that by choosing God, by connecting with him, you are making him happy?"

"No, I have never thought of that," she confessed.

"Not only are you making him happy, but you are bringing him glory. Through your connection to the Heavenly Father, you are not only receiving help, but you are receiving his glory."

Cindy wasn't sure she understood.

"Think of that light as a two-way connection," Mary continued. "You are both connecting with each other."

Cindy nodded.

"With every connection with God, there is a transference of some kind. The essence of who you are, your personality, and your giftings, and your friendship benefit the Lord. He enjoys you! And the fruit of the Spirit, friendship, and grace from God benefits you."

Cindy was starting to understand. "It is like we both bring something to the relationship. Together we are more than when we are apart."

"Exactly!" Mary agreed. "Now, the Lord is perfect and enough for you just as he is, but we are his creation, so connecting with him brings him joy." Mary paused to let that sink into Cindy's thinking. "You know what else?"

"What?"

"As the Lord fills you with his light, you become light to others. Others can find him and find freedom through the light that dwells in you."

"I never thought of it that way."

"Remember the lady at the grocery store?"

"Yes."

"You were God's light to her. Your smile of encouragement was more than just a smile, it was full of God's light. It broke through the darkness that was consuming her in that moment and allowed her to breathe and to function."

"I could see that," Cindy thought about the interaction with the grocery clerk. "Before I caught her eye, she was welling up with tears, and she was having difficulty knowing what to do. She seemed stuck."

"Yep."

"After we made eye contact, and I smiled at her, her face lightened. She almost immediately called the manager, and the situation was resolved."

"Exactly! Only the powerful light of the Lord can make such a big difference."

"Something else happened at that moment," Cindy noted.

"What was it?"

"Well, before I got in line – I think all my life really – I just thought nothing mattered. I remember thinking 'I don't care' so many times that day," she ran her finger along the seam of the couch as she put her thoughts together. "I think without having a purpose, I just didn't know what mattered." She looked up at Mary. "I didn't know what was important, or if I was important. Something about that exchange broke that for me. I think that's why I was even able to think about my purpose today."

"I think you are right, Cindy." Mary paused to allow Cindy to digest this new information. "So, your connection with God, your choosing to share his light in that moment, allowed the cashier to break through her own darkness and also changed your way of viewing life." She waited. "That is a powerful light!"

"And it is a powerful purpose," Cindy added.

"Yes, it is."

Cindy's mind was swirling and so was the darkness around the room. A portal had opened at that last revelation, and the entire angelic guard knew it was a matter of minutes before the darkness was forced back through the portal, away from this place and away from Cindy.

"I want to do that," Cindy started with a hint of confidence in her voice. "I want to choose to connect with God every day, and I want to choose to allow his light to connect with others through me."

"Even if it is something as simple as a smile?" Mary persisted.

"Is a smile really simple if the light of the Most High God is reaching through it to connect with someone?" Cindy asked with a wry grin.

Mary laughed.

"Yes, even if it is something small," Cindy confirmed.

"Would you like to tell the Lord?"

Cindy thought for a moment. Usually, Mary did the praying and Cindy would just agree with the prayers. Occasionally, Cindy would pray herself. After thinking for a moment, she realized this was one of those times. "Yes, I will do it."

They both bowed their heads. As Cindy opened her mouth to pray, light from Heaven burst into the room sending demons and dark entities all over the room scurrying for the dark cover of the portal.

"Dear God, thank you for showing me what it

means to have a purpose. I want the purpose you have given me. I want to connect with you and choose you every day. I want to allow your light to connect with others through me – even in small acts like a smile. I am honored you would choose me for this. Thank you for letting me see this. In Jesus' name, Amen."

As Cindy said Amen, one last shriek went up from the darkness, and just like that, it was all gone. There was no battle, there was no corralling. The presence of God activated by Cindy's choice to serve God with intentionality was so strong that the demons themselves chose to run away.

"That felt good," Cindy stated.

Mary smiled and paused briefly before deciding to wrap up the session, which had run over by about fifteen minutes.

When Cindy left the office and started her drive home, she could almost feel the light that was living inside of her. It was crazy to think it had been there all along, and she was only just now feeling it.

The weather outside was beautiful which made her drive all the better. The sun was shining, and the temperature was warming up. Cindy knew the night would bring more clouds and possibly rain, but she didn't care. She felt the warmth of her connection with the Lord, and she was thankful, so thankful that she chose him, and he chose her. She thought of so many times when God connected with someone around her through her smile, kind word, or a witness of his goodness, and the feeling of purpose filled her being. She was complete in him – even if she wasn't healed yet.

"The freedom she is receiving is powerful and will extend for many generations," Michael observed.

"Praise be to the Most High God," the angelic guard said in unison.

"Praise be!" they all echoed.

"What will happen to her parents?" Hezek inquired.

"That is outside of our responsibility," Michael replied. After a moment of thought he added, "only God knows the answer to that."

On the outskirts of town, in a beautiful, elegant farmhouse, a storm was brewing. "I am so sick and tired of things falling apart around here!" Darlene was angry and slamming cabinet doors.

"I'm so sorry ma'am." The slender woman wearing black pants and a neatly pressed white shirt stood at attention and listened as Darlene ranted and raved about all the mistakes made by catering staff over the years. "How can I fix this, ma'am," the young caterer asked when there was a lull in the chastisement.

Darlene was fiddling with the faucet now. "I'm quite certain it will never be fixed by someone like you." Her disdain for the woman sent a wave of black slime over the lady's body.

The young woman fought hard to maintain her professional posture, but the weight of the invisible slime was too much for her. One of her shoulders dropped just as Darlene turned to face her.

The prominent woman sighed with disgust. "Get out of here, just get out of here!" She waved her arm wildly as the young woman rushed out of the room with tears rolling down her face. "Last time I hire someone from that service." Darlene was muttering as she stormed out of the kitchen and stomped up the stairs.

Outside of the house, the vile black liquid had covered every square foot of grass, plants, and building. Lumps of stench and goo were in the trees and continuing to seep into the farmhouse. Darlene had made her choice, and tonight she was paying the price, as was everyone around her.

Chapter 13

It was Sunday, again. It seemed like these days rolled around more frequently than they used to. Cindy wasn't sure how that happened. As she sat at the little table in her kitchen staring out the window she debated going to church or staying home. Then the warmth from the session the day before washed over her.

"Father God, I want you to use the light you have placed in me to connect with someone else today," Cindy prayed.

A new hope for the day rose in her heart. Within forty-five minutes she had showered and dressed for church. With a travel mug full of coffee in her hand, she headed out the door curious to see what the Lord would do.

The church parking lot was as busy as usual. Cindy didn't seem to mind. She kept picturing the little seed of light in her heart reaching out and connecting to the Light of God. Then this brighter and stronger light, reached from her to touch the cashier. "That must have been what Daniel did for me," she thought. "The Light of God reached through him to help me." She smiled at the thought.

Her usual check of the church attendees from her hidden parking spot took only a few minutes. With her purse and keys in hand, she headed for the building. It was strange to not have Daniel there to greet her – or for her to avoid. She smiled again. She had only really seen him a few times, but his presence was so natural and welcoming that it felt like he had always been there.

The first safe man.

Safe? Someone questioned.

The safest one we have known.

The silence seemed to indicate internal agreement on that fact.

Inside the church, Angela was the first to notice her. "Hi Cindy!"

"Hi," Cindy responded with a slight smile.

Angela gave her a warm hug. "It is good to see you this morning."

Cindy was still smiling as she was imagining the Light of God in each of them connecting. It felt safe to connect with someone if it was the Light of God making the connection. There was something about that. She was protected and hidden in his light. It was the first time in her life that connection with another person didn't really seem all that dangerous. That was both wonderful and terrifying.

The worshiping angels in her entourage were fully engaged in the songs of those angels stationed around the church. This was a place where people of all kinds gathered and worshiped the Lord.

"Do you want to get coffee this week?" Angela asked.

"Sure," Cindy replied over her shoulder as she was making her way to her spot in the sanctuary.

The worship leader started the service with an up-beat tune sending worship to the Lord. Cindy stood and sang along as best she could. She didn't know many of the worship songs at church these days. So many of them were new, and she had missed a lot of church over the past two years. Her playlist at home was filled with her favorites, very few of which had been written in the past five years.

After worship, the pastor made a few announcements. He spoke briefly about Daniel and the memorial service that was held the day before. Cindy could feel a lump in her throat. She was surprised to be so emotional about it.

We didn't even know him. A voice reminded her.

Cindy swallowed the lump down as hard as she could and gave her head a small shake.

As the pastor began his sermon, he opened with the verse in Matthew 5:16 that says, "In the same way, let your light shine before others, so that they may see your good deeds and glorify your Father in heaven."

Cindy couldn't help but smile as she thought about the light she was shining. It was actually God's light, placed in her. She didn't need to do anything to have that light, and God connected that light to whomever he chose. She just needed to be available.

Beautiful, she thought.

As he continued preaching, he referred to Romans 11:36 which says "for from him and through him and for him are all things. To him be the glory forever. Amen." He talked about this being the "good works" that the previous verse talked about.

"Purpose," she said under her breath.

Funny how these verses held a whole new meaning to her today. Before she saw the seed of God's light in her, she would have thought her "good works" needed to be big things for God. Work that people would acknowledge and praise. Now she knew there was nothing further from the truth. It was the light of God through her that made her works good. That light made simple things like a smile bring God's light to people and glory to God.

Amazing, she thought.

As service ended, Cindy stood to leave. She saw a couple of kids run by out of the corner of her eye and instinctively turned to look. They were Daniel's kids. It looked like they were chasing a friend. She then saw their mom come up and coral them. Cindy had never met her before or any of Daniel's kids. She had only seen them with their dad once.

She watched them for a moment and the lump slowly began to build in her throat again. This time, the lump was much harder to swallow down. She began to move quickly to get to her car. Tears never used to come out in these situations, but with the amount of healing she had received, the tears could be quite unpredictable.

She made it to the car just in time.

That was close.

No tears fell that day, but the lump in her throat never left. She pushed away the thoughts of sadness and grief surrounding the loss of the red scarf man and went through the day focusing on the little seed of light in her.

As Monday came though, she realized that most of Sunday afternoon was a blur.

I'm not sure what happened yesterday, but today

we really need to focus, she thought to herself.

It is so sad.

What is sad?

It is sad to think of Daniel's family.

Cindy was surprised to hear the thoughts in her mind. She didn't even know his family. Why is this so difficult?

How do they move on? How do we move on?

It was too much for Cindy. The lump was growing in her throat again, and she could feel the tears burning in her eyes. She decided to shut down this thinking before it cost her another day of work.

* *

Cindy felt tears welling up in her eyes. The view of her lap was coming into focus. She recognized the green fabric of the couch in Mary's office.

I must be at therapy, she thought.

She squeezed her eyes shut briefly to hold back the tears as she looked up. Mary was jotting a note on her notepad, and then looked up. She greeted Cindy warmly.

"I don't know what happened," Cindy started. "What were we talking about?"

What happened to the week? She wondered.

Not again.

How much time did I lose? The whole week? She wondered.

Over the years, she had learned to just pick up wherever she was and move forward.

"Daniel's family," Mary reminded.

"Oh, yes, that's right," she paused to gather her thoughts. "I saw one of his kids at church this past weekend." She paused to think, "they were running through the lobby, maybe playing tag or being chased by another kid, I don't know."

Mary waited for the words to come to Cindy.

"I don't know. There was something about it. He seemed like a normal kid – just running through the church – but I know that isn't true. He isn't just a normal kid."

"What do you mean," Mary inquired.

"Well, his dad just died. His whole world is different now," Cindy could feel those tears again threatening to break through the barrier of her eyes, "his world must be shattered. How could he go on?"

Her tears were so strong now, like a tsunami coming towards the shore, held back only by the force of her will.

Mary waited, knowing there was more.

"I mean, it isn't like his dad is coming back. Isn't he sad? Is he mad? Devastated, that would be the word, his world will never be the same. You can't just move on from that, you can't!"

Cindy clamped her mouth shut. Her tears seemed to be building force with every word she said, and she was afraid she would burst if she continued.

"Cindy," Mary started as she leaned forward slightly in her chair, "you don't move on from something traumatic. Moving on implies leaving it behind. You move forward. One day at a time," she hesitated until Cindy's eyes met hers, "but I don't think this is about Daniel, is it?"

At that, the flood of tears erupted down Cindy's cheeks. She buried her face in her hands and sobbed with her whole body for several minutes. Mary waited silently.

The songs of worship to the Lord increased a bit as the worshiping angels recognized the work of the Holy Spirit in the room. It was a beautiful thing to see tears that had been restrained for so many years flow freely. An act of God's great mercy was on display.

As the tears began to subside, Cindy nodded in agreement with Mary's last statement.

"I just feel like I have lost so much in my life," she reached for a tissue as the tears continued to stream down her face, "I mean, I have basically lost my entire life. The thought of moving on, just forgetting all that has happened and moving on, seems…it seems…impossible." Cindy blew her nose. "I mean how is that even possible to do?"

"What does 'moving on' mean to you?"

"I don't know," Cindy thought for a moment as she continued to wipe the tears off her face, "I guess it means that you shake it off, you know, don't let it bother you, and just live your life."

"I wonder what Jesus would say about that."

Cindy knew what that meant. She closed her eyes and waited to see what the Lord would show her.

It only took a minute for a picture to begin to form in her mind.

She saw herself as an infant. She was smiling and crawling on the floor. The carpet was bright colors and seemed soft under her hands and knees. She thought how this might bring a smile to the face of most people, but she didn't smile. She knew too much about her horrific childhood. These pictures were not pleasant, but she persisted, waiting to see what the Lord would show her.

Soon, she could tell she was getting older. A toddler, a small child, a pre-teen, a teen, she was growing and changing. The trauma was no longer at the forefront of her mind. As she looked at the movie of her growth, it was the way she was changing that caught her attention. At first, she was growing in size, then her style was changing, after that she could see the maturity developing on her face and in her demeanor.

Each year that passed was part of her story, part of her life. She didn't leave behind her size or style or personality, she just grew and changed.

"What do you think it means?" Cindy asked Mary.

"I think there is more, let's wait on the Lord a little longer," Mary instructed.

Cindy complied and closed her eyes again.

Now she saw the same series of pictures, but this time it was overlaid with her academics. Learning to read, do math, write stories, do science, the list of academic milestones was normal enough. She was an average student. But in this picture, she saw these milestones differently. She could see how each one built on the other. She learned to add and subtract, which allowed her to learn fractions which lead to doing basic algebra and so on. Each skill was needed before she could move forward to the next skill. Just like with aging, it was all connected and necessary for growing.

Cindy froze in her seat, afraid of what was next.

A black shadow began to grow at her feet again. Michael stabbed his sword deep into the darkness. It didn't leave, but it stopped moving.

"Cindy," Mary said calmly, "are you ok?"

"I don't want it to be true," Cindy said without looking up.

"You don't want what to be true?"

"I'm afraid the next series of pictures will have my trauma story and it will all seem necessary and part of me just like my growth and my academics," her breath was staggered as she spoke. "I don't want that to be true." She cringed slightly; her eyes still closed.

"Cindy," Mary started. She paused waiting for Cindy to open her eyes, "I know this is a lot."

Cindy nodded. She was wiping her tears and blowing her nose. Then she sat, motionless, and waited for Mary to continue.

"How have the past two timelines felt?" Mary asked.

"Peaceful," Cindy replied without hesitation. "It was like they made sense of something; I just don't know what."

"Shall we give Jesus a chance to finish what He is showing you?"

Cindy nodded, still hesitant, but willing to proceed.

As she closed her eyes, she clutched the wadded Kleenex in her hand.

Michael still had his sword in the shadow

surrounding her feet. It had lessened in size, but it was still thick, and a slight rumble could be heard from it.

"What do you see?"

"I see the same timelines, my age, my academics, but now I have a backpack in the scenes." She waited as the picture developed in her mind. "I am putting things in my backpack and taking them out. Random items. A shoe, a notebook, a vase. It is like all the items being handed to me are my life experiences. Some are nice, some are dusty, some are broken. There are many different things."

"What stands out to you in the picture?"

"The writing utensils."

"Writing utensils." Mary echoed.

"Yes, crayons, pencils, pens, markers, chalk, all different kinds of writing utensils. Some I hold, and some I put away. As the timeline of my life plays, this is the most consistent of all the items in my backpack." With her eyes still closed, Cindy tilted her head.

Mary waited.

The thick cloud was starting to droop. Michael twisted his sword in a half-turn.

"Now the picture has shifted," Cindy paused as the new scene formed in her mind. Her body was more relaxed as her curiosity replaced her fear. "I see Jesus, He is with me, and we are using the writing utensils to write in a big book. I see my name on the front of the book, I think it is my story." She cringed again, but just for a moment. "Jesus said to just watch." Her shoulders relaxed again.

"Only the presence of God can make an impact like that," Ronan stated.

After a few minutes the dark cloud at Cindy's feet had dissipated and Michael was sheathing his sword. "The battle she was facing must be over."

"Praise be to the Most High God!" The group chanted loudly.

"Praise be!"

The glory of the Lord began to fill the room as Cindy opened her eyes. The voices of the worshiping angels were bold and strong and each of those in the angelic guard were bowed low to worship the Sovereign God.

Cindy moved slowly as she wiped her eyes one more time. There was a look of awe and wonder on her face.

"What did He show you?" Mary asked with a knowing smile on her face.

"It is hard to explain," Cindy could feel her body. She was in her body. This was an unusual feeling. She felt relaxed. Not happy or emotional, but just relaxed. This was also an unusual feeling.

"The book was my life story, but it wasn't about what happened to me, it was about who I was becoming, who I am becoming." She waited, still digesting what the Lord had shown her. "The different writing utensils represented all the different things that happened to me. Some were good, but most were not. Some were straight up evil. But what Jesus wrote with them," she pondered her words, "it didn't matter what the utensil was. It didn't matter if it was good or bad, he would have written the same thing. He would have written about who I am becoming," she was talking faster now, telling the story with her hands moving.

Her breath was deep and steady and there was a glint in her eye. "God made me, he is making me. Whatever happens to me, he uses it to write the story of me. The person he designed me to be all along."

Except for the worshipers, everyone in the room was quiet. The truth that was sinking into Cindy's soul and spirit was deep and powerful. It was God's truth.

"He is making me to be like him, kind, generous, trustworthy, bold, all of the things that Jesus is," she thought about it. "So many of those writing utensils were absolutely awful, you wouldn't even think they could write, but he wrote with them. He would write 'she will become bold' or 'she is growing in compassion for others.' He never wrote in my book what happened to me, although he knew. He felt the pain and sorrow of each bad memory, but that wasn't where he focused. That wasn't what he wrote about. Instead, he wrote who I was becoming."

"That's amazing, Cindy," Mary was smiling.

"Wait, I think He wants to show me something else," Cindy closed her eyes.

After a moment she opened them again. "It was from the vision He gave me a few months back," she started, "do you remember? The one with the DNA?"

"I remember," was all Mary said as she scribbled a note on her pad.

"The story is about what is happening with the strands of DNA designed and created by God. What they are becoming. We only see the darkness and evil and bad choices – the slime that surrounds the DNA more and more over time. BUT our experiences don't make up the story of who we are. He *uses* the experiences to write the story of who we are becoming!"

"That is beautiful! I love the way God designed us," Mary exclaimed.

"And the way he writes our story." Cindy was

thinking again, "you know, I always thought my life story was about all my experiences. If that is true, then you can't just move on. Your experiences are part of your identity. They make up who you are."

"How do you see it differently now?" Mary asked.

"Well, it isn't about *what happens*. It is about *who you are becoming*. Whatever life hands me, God uses it to write about how it is shaping me. So much of what happens in life grieves the Lord. He cried when he pulled a few of the writing utensils out of my bag, but it was like he was determined not to let the bad utensil keep him from writing. It was like he was doing something big, and he would make it work. It didn't matter if it was a crayon, a pencil, or a piece of chalk. In fact, I think He would have written the same story regardless of what happened to me because He always knew who I would become."

"That sounds a lot like Romans 8:28," Mary commented.

Cindy knew that verse well. She never liked it, but Mary used it a lot. It had to do with God working everything out for good. It had always seemed weird and impossible, but today it was making sense.

Mary continued, "While God doesn't want trauma and bad things to happen, your experiences can't stop you from becoming who God designed you to be. When you gave your life to Him, it ensured your future – not just your future in heaven – but it ensured your identity in Christ. It ensured who you were becoming regardless of your experiences."

"Amazing." Cindy stated, still in awe of what the Lord was showing her. "I think I understand the vision better from last fall. I now know the importance of walking with the Lord and drawing close to Him. As He cleans and heals my own life, He is cleaning and healing my DNA. He was writing the story all along, I just needed to cooperate. I need to trust Him. More people should know this."

"It is a powerful re-frame on our life as believers," Mary observed. "I will be curious to see what happens with this new insight this week."

Cindy knew it was time for the session to wrap up. "I will be curious as well," she said with a smile.

As Cindy left session that day, she felt lighter. The weight of all the evil things that had happened throughout her life was shifting in a way she could not put into words. To think God was writing the story of who she would become all along, well, it was so redeeming!

Michael and the angelic guard in his lead followed her to the car and made their usual route of going before and coming behind her. They were accustomed to her routine as they had been with her for many years, but as she was healing some things were beginning to change.

A few months ago, Cindy had started taking longer drives after sessions and sometimes during the week. She had found a couple of coffee shops she enjoyed visiting, and sometimes she would drive through the country and just look at the trees and countryside. The angels assigned to her were now a little more alert of her movements and were adapting to her newfound freedom. Today's drive though would take her somewhere quite unexpected.

As she drove, music played quietly on the radio. The weather was becoming more tolerable. Warmer days were moving in, and winter was moving out. Some of the trees in the small country town were beginning to bud and the song of the birds was becoming a more regular part of the day.

Her little Toyota seemed to have a mind of its own today as she drove, winding and weaving to the edge of town and into the country. It didn't take long for Michael to realize where they were headed.

"Kaleb, take two warriors and head to the driveway entrance," he looked ahead of the car as he spoke, "I don't know what she has in mind, but we want to be ready." Michael turned to Hezek, "trail behind a bit to make sure we don't pick up any stragglers. I will handle things here in the car."

The huge black portal over Cindy's childhood home was now visible in the distance. It was difficult to know what was going through her mind. In the past, different parts of Cindy had taken over and driven out to visit her parents out of a twisted sense of loyalty. It had been a long time since that had happened.

Michael addressed one of her ministering angels who was in the car with her, "Salih, how are things?"

"She seems fine. I feel the Holy Spirit here with us."

"I do as well," Michael concurred. "Let me know if anything changes."

As the car moved towards the family property, Cindy's demeanor seemed relaxed. Her finger was tapping on the steering wheel to the beat of the song on the radio.

A small group of worshippers had joined Zral and Abel who were singing praises to the Most High God.

"Interesting," Michael observed.

When they were within a half block of the farmhouse driveway, Cindy pulled over on the side of the road. The dirt and rocks briefly kicked up around the car as she came to a stop. She took a deep breath and closed her eyes.

"Father God, I have been connected to this home and this family for way too long. I know today that you are doing something new in me," she paused as she thought about her words. "Actually, it isn't a new thing. You have been doing it all along." She smiled. "I choose the story you are writing about who I am becoming, and I reject the story that my family tried to write about me."

At that, the angels heard a loud burst come from the family house. Four dark spirits hovering near Cindy's car appeared and were instantly swept into the driveway and deep onto the property.

"Something is happening," Kaleb reported from the edge of the driveway. "I can't be sure, but it seems the portal is backed up. Evil that was once going out from this place is now pouring back onto the land."

"Is it being restrained?" Michael asked.

Kaleb looked again. "I'm not sure, but it doesn't seem to notice we are here."

"That is good!" Michael responded. "This is a strong indication of the mighty power of God in breaking off the ties between Cindy and this land."

"Praise be to the Most High God!" the angels

shouted.

"Praise be!"

Michael noticed the chain he had seen in session a few weeks back was becoming visible. It lay on the ground stretching from the car to the driveway, and it disappeared into the darkness of the property.

In the car Cindy was still expressing her heart to the Lord, "thank you for protecting me all of these years from things I didn't even know about," a few tears had started to run down her face. Her body was still relaxed and the need for Salih was very minimal. Her emotions were flowing more easily than they had in a long time.

Cindy took a deep breath and then relaxed again as she closed her prayer, "I trust you to continue to disconnect me from any other ties to this place. I trust you to disconnect me from my parents." She glanced up at the property. The house where she was raised stood just out of sight behind the tall evergreens that lined the road on either side of the driveway.

"She is feeling the pull to her parents," Salih started. "No wait," he paused for a moment. "I think she is feeling compassion for them."

Michael nodded. "She has the heart of her Heavenly Father. There is no false loyalty there, only compassion."

"I trust you with the future of both of my parents," Cindy continued. "You know what is best for them. It isn't my place to say."

Cindy started her car and put it into drive.

"We are leaving," Michael informed the angels who were stationed behind and before her, "Hezek, you and your troops stay behind for a few moments to make sure nothing follows. Kaleb, proceed ahead to ensure safe passage wherever she may be going."

"As I pull away from this property," Cindy was saying as the car moved back onto the road, "let this be an indication of me leaving all that has happened here behind, in Your hands, Father God. Please take me to the place where you want me to be. Please continue to write the story of who I am becoming."

At that, the shackle on her angle broke open. Michael picked up the broken end with the tip of his sword and threw it onto the defiled land.

An incredible peace settled over the car as the Holy Spirit's presence became tangible to Cindy, as well as her angelic guard. Holy reverence for the work the Lord was doing permeated the group as the little Toyota pulled away from the farmhouse drive. With each country block separating her from the evil of her past, Cindy began to feel more and more free. Her decision to accept the writing of her story by the Lord had moved her into a new place of peace and healing.

What does this mean for us? Someone inside inquired

I don't know, Cindy thought in response to them, *but whatever it means, I know we will be together.*

How do you know, the little voice responded.

I know because God made me, He made you, and He is writing the story of who we will become. You are a part of that story, we all are.

Cindy thought about that for a few moments. While her experiences were important, they were no longer the focus. God knew who he made her to be, and she would become that person. She knew that now. He would use whatever life handed her to ensure she became all she was made to be. He had been fighting for her healing and growth since before she even knew she needed him to.

A smile crossed her face. It turns out her war strategy wasn't about what she could do for God, it was about what God had been doing for her all along.

"And I can't wait to see what you will do next!"

BOOK ONE:
MORE THAN MEETS THE EYE

BOOK TWO:
WAR STRATEGY

COMING SOON!

BOOK THREE:
WHOLENESS

For more information visit: www.melissafinger.com